The
Ramblings
of a
Small-
Town
What's-His-Name
C. K. Conners

PUBLISHING®

Contents

CRITICS ARE RAVING!

"Don't expect this to be what you expect it to be, unless you expect it to be like a good, 32-tooth cavity drilling sans anesthetic."

Ringo Raul D'Rossi / *Senior Snoot, Snooty's Quarterly*

"I have heard tell of other, more insufferable works in the offing, guaranteed to challenge one's cache of curses, as well as one's posture. Has he no mercy?"

Mike Roe Skäpik / *Executive Sycophant, The Backseat Blogger*

"The stories are nice, I suppose; but each prologue contained within should come with a complementary sedative or hot water bottle for the head. Such would be only human decency."

Sam Pulsyze / *Author,* Rite-Syze: The Food Sample Kiosk Diet

---

"I plan to pursue legal action against the author."

Kit N. Caboodle / *Planner at Dee Sasster Event Planning*

"If rumors of upcoming novels are to be trusted, I fear this collection is but a taste of the horrors Conners is soon to unleash upon the minds and spines of the literary world."

Aunt C. Pantzy / *Aunt Catherine Pantzy's Tranquil Living Hour, ZoneOut TV*

"I give the entire array a solid 4.5 out of five stars, as its presentation was not only pleasing and its offering aromatic, I also found each morsel even more savory than the last. Most satisfying! I shall return again and again, for such exquisite [writing] is rarely discovered—I dare say but once in ten lifetimes!"

Brian

[Full disclosure: While this review had indeed been submitted for the text, it is believed to have been erroneously done and intended for the truly delightful Italian restaurant down the street. Either way, we're takin' it!]

"Conners has threatened to publish novels. Is there any way to stop him?"

Ivana Keith-DeCook / *Partner at the Law Offices of Keith, Mee, & Thayuluvme*

Introduction

It's time you knew the truth.

IT is a secret long kept among those in the literary world that to tell a story or compose a narrative is a task, due to its understood responsibility, most agreeably shouldered with company. There are limitations, of course. Take, for instance, the kitchen. Speaking as an olive on the proverbial Sicilian olive branch that is part of my ethnic configuration, I can tell you that should the number of cooks operating the spices, sauces, and sassy say-so-ing in the kitchen ever exceed the sacred number of two (and even that might be pushing it), ladles and meatballs may begin to take flight. Why do you think authentic Italian restaurants with bona fide Italian chefs serve a nearly all-Italian customer base? Other patrons are scared away due to a lack of cultural understanding and experience. Should you, dear reader, be a non-Italian frequenter of or casual diner in Italian restaurants, you are indeed a brave soul and no doubt a good bound or two out of your head insane. The law of averages is sure and soon to catch its prey. May heaven help you.

Steering back to my desired course of thought, the same principle that ensures relative peace and stabilized personalities in Italian kitchens can be applied with efficacy to the composing of a literary work, particularly a novel. We see it all the time: a novel with two authors, a children's book with words and illustrations penned non-ambidextrously by different hands, or when an author, typically one with a chest devoid of its main, ventricle organ, or a head equal in size and constitution to a blimp, enlists the aid of one to whom he offers no credit: a ghostwriter. One-man bands do exist; even the author of this book has flown solo on a novelic (new word, Webster; pronounced *no-vel-ick*) project or two. However, such ambitious fools, who enjoy tugging clumps of hair from the old coconut and banging the bean repeatedly against the drywall, are not the topic of this little piece.

What, then, I can hear you ask, *is the point thou art trying to make, Mr. Conners?*

Mr. Conners?

No.

Not Mr. Conners.

Mr. Narrator.

I can sense some confusion. Even now, as I write this piece in preparation for publication, I can feel—literally feel—the weight of all the raised eyebrows, cocked heads, and collective, bewildered tongues lifting in unison a high-pitched, *Whaaat?*

No, I am not C. K. Conners. I am his narrator, his employee: a self-proclaimed literary maestro in my own right, screened and trusted by him whose name graces the cover of this book, charged with delivering to you, dear reader, that which he designs for his expression and your entertainment.

You may think this irregular.

An author hiring a narrator to do his storytelling? What next? Drivers who entrust the steering and pedaling to a computer? Surgeons who dictate incisions to a set of hired hands? Scripted reality television?

I'll admit, it does seem a trifle odd; but remember what I told you before: authors have for centuries shared the joy of storytelling with others. It is only logical. One man (the author) composes the story: the ins and outs, as well as the detailed blueprints for the development of characters, settings, plot devices, and the overall telling of the tale. And the other man (the narrator) studies that blueprint, and brings it to life upon the page.

Don't be disappointed. This is very common. Mr. Conners and I are just bringing a classic, sub rosa practice into the light. Look at some of your favorite and least favorite books. I know for a legally unprovable fact that nearly all of your favorite authors do not solely compose every piece of narration on which they stamp their names. And the ones that do, the ones who think they're above the hiring of a professional raconteur, give us such gems as *The Hoary Hue of the Billionaire*, or *My Baby-Free Maternity Leave*.

Pray tell, you pose (rather eloquently, I might add), *wherefore, should thine employer possess the virtues of a generous ventral organ, or a head inflated not with swelling egotism, doth thy name appear nowhere upon the binding of this humble publication?*

A good question. A tad loquacious, but I—as you will see throughout the course of our acquaintance—am not one to try such a tongue. Indeed, it would seem that, since the name Conners is the only one that appears upon the jacket, I am nothing more than a ghostwriter, giving away the best sentences, paragraphs, and phrases of my life, to only be cast aside, used and vacant, broken and without credit.

I will not say I am content, though such does not mean I harbor any discontent. The fact is this: the complexion of a true narrative artist, like me, seeks neither fame nor recognition; and should my work demand recognition, should it be so removed from the author's voice that it becomes obvious that two voices are employed in telling the tale, then I have not done my job.

Have you ever read a book in which the story is better than the writing? Or the story is pure garbage, but the writing is superb? So have I; and such cases are evidence of a dysfunctional author-narrator relationship. These are like the fish in love with the sparrow, or the sweetheart you had convinced yourself you were going to marry back in your high school days. They never work out in practice. Without a comprehensive screening process, which takes time and patience, the author who rushes into a literary partnership with a narrator he does not fully understand, and with whom he has not bonded aright, is liable to find (perhaps expose is a better word) something defining and indispensible deep within, something inherent to each party, that will act as a monkey wrench, eventually blowing the entire work to pieces.

It took years for Mr. Conners' and my paths to cross. He had long hesitated at the idea of taking on a narrator; he believed his voice was strong enough. But the day we met, when our hands bumped as we both reached for the last pad of blank paper at the supplies store, just before those same hands turned into fists that swiftly met the other's eye, something inside, inside both of us, knew, beyond a shadow of a doubt, that destiny had finally called.

Now, it has never been proven, but some say that Mr. Conners had merely reached for a pad of paper that was situated beside a giant mirror, and that, after a glance into it and a subsequent violent start and recoil that saw his hand fly into his own eye, he had bonded with the figure staring dumbly back at him and holding his own recently poked eye. Even I ponder my own actuality every once in a while. It is, in fact, rather curious that he and I should bear identical ethnic backgrounds, possess hair of the same hue, variety, and population per square area; are almost indistinguishable in our mannerisms (though I say *his* are distinctly more insufferable than my own), and even share a birthdate.

The point, however, is this: Mr. Conners and I are of one mind. Is that mind the same, physical mind? I'll leave that to the professionals presently observing me through a thick, glass window (*wink*). Nevertheless, this is the way it is.

And so, now that we have gotten introductions out of the way, allow me to tackle the job my employer had asked that I complete in fewer than five hundred words (Ha! Like *that* was ever going to happen), and welcome you to *The Ramblings of a Small-Town What's-His-Name*: a collection of short stories, composed entirely by C. K. Conners. Yes, you read correctly: these works are purely of Mr. Conners' hand. I narrate only the long-winded intermissions between stories.

You're not narrating? Thank goodness! But for what, then, was all this I'm-the-narrator-not-the-Author *business?*

Simple. The Author wanted me to introduce myself. He said that since I am employed in the narrating of several of his novels (which are presently awaiting publication), he wanted to expose me to the populous, so as to avoid having to insert my introduction in what are already lengthy books. He knew and knows, as I did and do, that had I been left to offer my salutation to the world in one of his novels, the book would find itself top-heavy with a novella-length piece about myself that played no part in the driving of the plot to its climax. Since this is a jigsaw of stories, he felt it was the perfect opportunity for me to say hello.

And I quite agree.

Hello, dear reader.

Now that you and I have been acquainted, you are ready to dive into *The Ramblings of a Small-Town What's-His-Name*. Seven stories lie in the offing, as well as eight more diversions from me, during which I shall endeavor to entertain and enlighten, as I provide you with insights as to the inspirations behind each piece.

And now, without further ado, I bid thee welcome to *The Ramblings of a Small-Town What's-His-Name*.

Let's get to it!

Prologue: Dancer

THIS is no way to begin. Not that I think *Dancer* is A bad story to kick off this collection—on the contrary. What I mean is that these little preambles are, as I said in the introduction, supposed to feature a few tidbits regarding the inspiration(s) behind each piece. However, I have no idea what had inspired this piece! The Author and I had discussed it during preparations for this book, but whatever he'd said has absolutely escaped me! I've put in a call to the Author. Hopefully he'll get back to me before I'm through writing this.

These prefaces, or intermissions, or whatever you want to call them (call them *zappadoos*, if you like; I don't care), have not been written in sequential order. The following *zappadoo* was written first, actually. And now that—

Hang on a minute. It's the telephone.

Hello?

It's the Author—if you could just keep it to a low roar for a moment, dear reader, that'd be great. Thanks.

Yes, sir. Thanks for call—

Uh huh.

Actually, no; I'm not even remotely interested in hearing about your evening. I'd rather we—

No, but—

Fine. So, you got to the restaurant, *and...?*

Uh huh.

What? Are you kidding? That's disgusting!

The lady behind you orders a tofu salad (*as if that's not disgusting enough*) and she's served a bowl of greens mixed by the chef's karate-chopping *toes?*

And you're *still* there?

What did you order?

Are you *crazy?*

Of course he's crazy! I knew that!

After what you saw, you ordered a salad?

Dare I ask what kind of salad?

A Caesar salad; okay. And what did you get?

The waiter grabbed the woman's tofu salad and gave it to you?

What kind of a place is this? Tell me you didn't eat that tofu mess.

You ordered a decaf. Sounds harmless enough…but I'm assuming it's not.

Oh, my goodness. You order decaf and they bring you veal. Of course they did.

You know what; as crazy as that place is, it has sure offered some useable material. I think we might be able to insert some of that into our current project.

What's the name of the restaurant—I want to be sure I never accidently go there.

The Puncake House…oh, brother.

Anyway, thanks for calling me back. I need to talk to you about *Dancer*.

What do you mean *Dan who?*

No! Your story! *DANCER!*

Right. What exactly do you want me to say about it?

You'll text it to me? Why not just tell me now?

Seriously? The busboys just converged on the same table, causing a three-busser pileup, and it's your job to attend to the injured passengers? Why not leave it to the waiters?

Well, what on earth are they waiting—no; you know what? I don't care. Just text me when you're able.

Sorry about that, dear reader (and by *that* I mean the parade of cringe-worthy jokes you've just endured—they were so bad, I'm sure you'll need an ice pack for all those *crinjuries* you've sustained...okay, that was the last one; I promise). Thank you for standing by so patiently.

New text from Crazy Kooky Conners*

*Let's have a look, shall we?

It reads: *"A fixation with the reality of loss."*

Right! Now I remember! Of course!

That conversation we'd had—it's all coming back to me: his wrinkled shirt; the seven-day stubble painted across his face; the overwhelming smell of body spray, undoubtedly applied to mask his natural perfume: a stale concoction, organically brewed in isolation, emanating from various bodily crevices; the manner in which he would flinch and gaze with wide, quavering eyes and trembling hands tapping his muttering lips whenever the sun would peek from behind the overcast sky; how he seemed to worship the energy drink and PBJ sandwich I'd placed before him, what with all the petting of the sweating can (an understandably nervous beverage) and the seemingly intoxicating, long sniffs he took of the bread; and his almost incessant use of the word "unexpected."

What I have just described, what I had until now successfully blocked out of my mind with fortified walls of desperate ignorance and severe, conscious neglect, was a meeting for which the Author had called upon completion of a week of isolated brainstorming and writing: a stint during which *Dancer* was born.

Having emerged from his hole, after seven days of intense concentration and composition, the Author called and then presented me with the products of his self-quarantine, of which there was more than just writing.

My nose was the first to receive the fruits of his labor. A noisome gas assailed and overran the olfactory organs the second I'd opened the door to his office, where he sat amid a yellowish haze. A gift for my gustatory nerves was soon after presented: a healthy sampling of a damp, warm, and delightful (should one be a dung beetle) smorgasbord of fermented human effusions to bless my tongue. Delicious.

Since I was without my WWI, standard-issue gas mask, I invited my employer to step into the foyer, where we might discuss his progress amongst the light and the living, preferably before my brain melted beneath the atmosphere and my eyes sizzled into ash. Accepting my invitation, he rose from the haze, at which point my watering eyes unpacked their share of the spoils.

I have alluded to several elements of his physical appearance in the above; however, I wonder if you've ever seen a set of trousers actively struggling to flee from the appendages to which they are attached. It must have been some time after day three that these pants had begun their desperate fight for freedom, because the way each pant leg swung heavily, as if it had perspired an Olympic swimming pool's worth of sweat during its quest for exodus, demonstrated clearly that these poor slacks must have had been struggling for several days. I even faintly recall hearing them call to me for deliverance.

Once I'd regained command over my sensationally over-stimulated faculties, had situated the Author into an armchair near an open window and an industrial-strength fan blowing outward, and had supplied him with liquid energy and basic sustenance, I inquired about his recent descent down the evolutionary ladder. Laughing off what was not entirely (but still in no small way) a serious question, he told me how—after days of etching the details and carefully crafting the blueprints for a three-book project on which we are currently working—a spark ignited in his brain. Given the atmosphere of his office, I was surprised the whole place hadn't gone up in flames as a result.

This spark, he said, had motivated him so immensely that he'd plunged into a sea of thought, and there remained for twenty-four hours. One could argue, as I often do, that such a prolonged submergence might have cost his brain necessary oxygen, thus leading to the rather *non compos mentis* artist we know today—but that's beside the point.

After a great deal of pondering this spark, he'd emerged with one word: "unexpected."

He was fascinated with this word. I can't tell you how many times he'd said it, partly because after the roughly thirtieth time he'd done so I'd commenced banging my head against the wall. I'm sure I'd blacked out and missed at least one or two of them. At any rate, this word, and the spark that had produced it, a spark he called, "A fixation with the reality of loss," became our first story in this collection: *Dancer.*

Before you go, dear reader, know that I had been cautioned against making the prologues for stories like *Dancer* too light-hearted, as these are not comic tales. However, knowing Conners like I do, I felt it would be best to ensure your experience is not a series of exhausting highs or a procession of discouraging lows, but rather an emotional rollercoaster of sorts.

Let's hope I'd judged rightly.

Proceed!

Dancer

"Thank you for coming."

I sit down in the chair across from his. Outside the wind is passing noiselessly by, but the rain patters against the windows like a herd of little school children racing to the playground at recess. It's late, after hours in most places. I guess offices like these are always open, though. Some things never sleep.

***

A bride never forgets her wedding day. Most women, if not all women, spend a large portion of their lives preceding that special day imagining and fanaticizing about every little detail, from the dress to the flowers. Really, no detail in a wedding can be considered small, nor can a woman be easily convinced to alter or amend that which she has since her youth constructed in her mind: that ideal day; her own special occasion. Everything must be perfectly set in place, carefully planned out, so that no last-minute surprises throw a monkey wrench into the cogs set in motion by the painstakingly produced blueprint of the proceedings.

Personally, I'd feared the unexpected. I always had. That over which I had no control, that which lies unseen, that which creeps unnoticed into one's path, causing a jarring detour—these are the things that would leave me wide awake at night and in a cold

20

sweat whenever I would ponder what lay beyond the next inevitable turn in life. However, not all unexpected events or details are unhappy or frightening in the end. And one may discover, as I have, that, not unlike the rush one experiences when leaping from a rocky cliff into the crystal pool below, the fear that steals one's breath away is really the first step toward the realization of something incredibly wonderful, and the breath that is taken away is truly breath worth letting go.

My husband and I met unexpectedly. I was young, though flirting with the age at which a woman is regarded as one who is destined for lifelong maidenhood. A woman wholly and contentedly devoted to her career, one might say.

I have heard it said that life will sometimes throw one a lemon. Should life be so "generous" as to do so, one is encouraged to make lemonade. I suppose this hurling is life's way of trying to get one's attention, to demonstrate to the beneficiary that that lemon, however jarring, can be the first ingredient in the recipe that will yield the key to said beneficiary's happiness. A lemon taken upside the head may not feel so great at present, but the prospects may be promising.

Well, life hadn't thrown any lemons at me that day, though it did throw lemonade *on* me. Actually, in all fairness, it was my soon-to-be husband who had done the deed. You see, it was summer, and I was just on my way out from the local coffee house, toting a diabetes-special lemonade, when, as I turned a blind corner on my way back to the office, I was met with the broad body of a man, which, as he and I collided, sent my sugary refreshment streaming down my chest. A rather impressive mess it was, with the icy liquid beginning its collision course with my body at the neck, and then, as if it had a mind of mischief, running a wide and branching path beneath my blouse, soaking everything from within. The stickiness that ensued only added to the magnificence of the mess.

Though I had tried my hardest to don a stern face and dig my heels resolvedly into an indignant mood, something inside of me could not help but accept the unexpected stranger's barrage of apologies. Maybe it was the way he'd declared, "Good heavens!," as we collided, or perhaps it was his choice of the words, "Dear me, miss," before beginning his apologetic bombardment. I suppose it could also have been the peculiar rush of being whisked away from my impending impact upon the ground by his powerful arms, or the gentle manner with which his strong hands repositioned me back on my feet, as if I weighed nothing at all. Possibly it was that I found amusement with the way he frantically, though rather gracefully, extracted a clean handkerchief with which I could dab myself relatively clean, and scooped up all my belongings, doing it all in an instant.

Unexpected. There's really no better way to put it. Everything about my life, our life, from that point forward was unexpected. I wasn't looking to introduce someone into my perfectly functional existence, solitary though it may have been. And I wasn't expecting to do so as willingly as I did. After that first hour with him, I had forgotten all the reasons why I'd wanted to remain alone, unopened to anyone.

Every day with him was unexpected. The sheer number of fascinating things that made up his very essence was beyond comprehension. And the ways in which he took fascination with me was probably the most unexpected thing of all. He took sincere interest in those parts of me I had believed were irrelevant, boring—worthless, basically. He made them special, not just for himself, but also for me. He made me see there was value in who I was, who I am.

Our evenings were unexpected, too. No dinner and movie nights, or long walks on short beaches, as go the clichés of romance. Instead we explored the world around us, leaving our comfort zones behind as we tasted new foods, met new people, climbed new heights, and sang through the streets of the city, as if we were the only two people in the world. And we danced. He was a magnificent dancer—lighter than air and full of balletic grace. He showed me how to fly. We danced to the beating of our hearts and the motion of the earth. We danced with meaning, with passion, with purpose. We danced beautifully.

A woman usually knows when the knee is about to bend, but the day he offered me a promise took me by surprise. And let's not forget that most beautiful symbol he then placed on my eager finger—not the flashiest or the grandest of tokens, but unexpectedly perfect. An unexpected rain fell over our outdoor, country ceremony; and though such would dampen the spirits of many, we found it unexpectedly heavenly. To dance as one in the rain—I'll never forget the feeling.

But unexpected is not always a pleasant experience. In time, the odds are bound to catch up.

***

"I'm afraid I have bad news. Please, sit down."

I know this kind of scene all too well. Every time I enter such an office as this I am reminded of that morning years ago. It was clear and sunny that day, though the news we were about to receive would turn our day into night. This time the world seems to be aware of what is to come. It's been raining all day.

"The damage is great. Irreversible, I'm afraid."

I'm not ready for this.

"You must convince him to stop."

Please stop talking.

"One scenario is bad, the other…"

This was unexpected.

***

We were preparing to start a family when the world made its descent into darkness. We'd talked long and with tremendous excitement about our desire to bring as many children into the world as we could. Unfortunately, and unexpectedly, our ability would be impaired.

The world interfered first. Turmoil erupted on foreign soil, and my husband answered the call to action, postponing our plans, at least (so we'd thought—hoped, rather) for a little while. I wrote to him every day, and he wrote to me, as he was able. I missed him so. In my letters I talked of home, and of the things he wanted and needed most to remember, the things that would keep him going through those dark and terrible days. And then, unexpectedly, I received word that our family was about to begin. I wrote to him immediately; and thankfully, and unexpectedly, he was able to return home for a four-week leave eight months later.

Words cannot express what I felt when I was once again in the arms of the one I love most after so much time apart spent worrying and praying for his safety. What lay ahead should have been a most wonderful, memorable time in our lives; but, as it turned out, it was only memorable—and unexpected.

It was a sunny morning the day we found out. What should have been a routine check turned into an unfathomable nightmare. Great danger was foreseen, and to avert what lay ahead, immediate action was needed. I was admitted that day. They tried everything, and we never gave up hope—not until that cold, lifeless, ever so tiny body was laid in my arms.

We spent the remainder of his leave in silence. No exploring. No singing. And no dancing. Just sitting in silence, watching with dead eyes as the world passed us by, one tick and tock at a time.

The day came when I again had to say goodbye. It was harder that time. Much harder. Even now I wonder how they'd managed to pry my fingers from his jacket. I couldn't be alone. Not then. Not ever again. I needed him more than ever. But life had other plans—unexpected plans.

***

"Thank you, doctor."

The words leave my lips, ever so softly, as I drift trancedly toward the door. My body moves at a despondent pace, independent of my conscious mind. I am preoccupied with visions of a happy past: a time when to experience the unexpected was to feel alive, to know the limitless heights above existence. Not like now. No, the unexpected now echoes only words of darkness through my mind, making me like the dead.

It's almost midnight. I haven't driven far, though I have driven long. The long drive makes me think of how we'd lived life up to this point, my dearest and me. We haven't gone far, and unlike most youth who live fast, we'd preferred to take our time with the dance, savoring every dip and glide and pirouette. I can think only of him, and what I know lies in the offing.

I pull my car up to the studio. It's a fantastic place—small but perfect. His car is parked out front, just as I knew it would be. There was no sense in going home to find him. If he'd received the same news that I had earlier today—and I know he did—there is no place else in the world he would be.

I enter through the side door and climb the stairs to the track above the dimly lighted floor. Down below, donning the outfit he'd worn the year we were married, when he'd led a dazzling performance on the biggest stage in the country, a performance that would have propelled his career had there never been a war, is my beloved husband. And he's dancing—dancing like I've never seen him dance before, as if he knows this is his last time. It is a spectacular, beautiful thing to behold.

But I can see every step he takes causes him great pain. I can see the beads of sweat pouring over his furrowed brow and down his trembling cheeks. His face contorts every time that one leg touches the floor. His wounds never fully healed. His heart cannot beat as it once did, not with the scar it bears from his time overseas. His knee cannot support him, not with all it lacks in composition after the charge that had ended his career in the service. I know the doctor warned him as he did me. But I know—I know more than I can bear—that my precious husband would rather see this world pass away than to have his wings forever clipped and be, until the end of his days, forbidden from ever again occupying the skies.

He moves with such grace, such elegance, even though I can see his eyes weeping from the pain. Strength and confident resolve are painted on his face. The floor rattles and the room echoes with thunderous pounds as he entrechats and brisés from left to right, then pirouettes and fouettés, over and over, each time on his wounded leg. And then, closing tight his eyes, my husband races across the floor before taking a powerful, beautiful, grand jeté leap through the air.

Time slows as he glides through the dim space, and I can see on his face a look of assuaging forfeit, of peaceful release. He knows, as I do, that this is his last flight.

My fingers cling to the railing as I gaze at him from above. I cannot speak. I cannot move. I can only watch as the man I love crouches on one knee, panting, taking in quivering, deep breaths to meet the pain. And then he looks up. He sees me, here, on the track. He regards me as if he knew I'd been here the whole time, watching his last dance. And he smiles, the same way he did every morning, every day we spent together, every hour of our unexpected lives, even in the days when the unexpected had brought more tears than shrieks of joy.

He smiles at me. And, as a tear falls from my eye, I smile back at him: my husband, my partner, my lover, and my friend.

Our dance has reached its end.

And what a beautiful dance it was.

Prologue:
And The Rain
Continued To Pour

ASK any true artist what message his or her work is meant to convey, and they will most often reply that whatever meaning the piece holds for them, the composer, is irrelevant to the meaning derived by its observer. Some artists can even be rather cagy about that which had inspired them to compose a particular piece in the first place, believing such information may influence the minds of their audience, and thus hamper what genuine emotion or natural experience might have been had. It is very true that art can produce meaning that goes beyond the intentions or imagination of the composer; and while I would never wish to discourage or impede such a revelational experience, I do feel that the artist's meaning is just as valid and equally important, and that, sometimes, a bit of context or brief anecdote can be enriching.

If you, dear reader, would like to experience the next piece, or any subsequent piece, free of these prefacing details, I invite you to skip ahead to the story, and then come back upon completion to receive this short account regarding its inspiration.

Sticking around?

Back from reading?

Great.

Let's proceed.

And The Rain Continued To Pour was first written in 2013, during what was arguably a forgettable year for the Author. Much was in decline at this stage in the Author's life—though comparatively to the rest of the seven billion people on the planet, he counted whatever misfortunes he'd experienced as blessings.

Feeling as though his creativity was suffering immensely due to circumstances, he took a walk on a warm, cloudy afternoon to clear his head. Strolling through his little town, he passed a small patch of green, situated beside a quiet brook, upon which sat several crescent, stone steps, each with an arch larger than its neighbor's (a rainbow-like design), as well as an abandoned gazebo. He did not approach the steps; he just gazed at them from a distance.

And then it began to rain.

A gentle rain it was, at first. The cool drops pattered about his feet, kicking up steam from the heated asphalt below, while the sound of tiny splashes played before him.

Prior to leaving his house, the Author had taken his MP3 device that he might listen to some soothing music as he walked. And it was then, as the rain intensified, that a certain song began to play: *Undan Hulu* by Ólafur Arnalds.

The Author had been introduced to the Icelandic composer by an old friend just a few years prior; and he had enjoyed his music so much that he purchased nearly every album available. He had heard this particular song several times before, but never had it felt so perfectly placed. It was so fitting, so precise; and as it played, the Author could see a vivid, moving scene playing before him on the stone steps. That night, as he lay in bed, he typed the forthcoming story into his MP3 player, as the song played in his head.

What was penned into the final form you are about to read is not rooted in any particular experience had by the Author. What befalls the focal character reflects not a memory, but rather the personification of a complex collection of emotions harbored even to this day.

For the Author, the meaning of the words *Undan Hulu* remains a mystery. It's not that he lacks the resources to discover it, but rather that those words have for him taken on a meaning he knows is most likely very different from the one to which they have been assigned. Revealing those words in their true form, as with nearly every title from Ólafur Arnalds' work, would serve only to raze the passion and significance he has already found. The Author is not one to advocate ignorance—on the contrary. However, for this piece and trivial instance, not knowing means far more than knowing.

It comes to me, now, that I have failed to insert any of my particular brand of levity into the above. It's not like me to go more than five paragraphs without tossing in a lighthearted joke or sarcastic comment. The Author has requested that I keep my own rambling to a minimum, as you, dear reader, have opened the covers of this book specifically to read his. However, since I have final review privileges for this work (the Author will not be seeing my contributions until *after* publication—talk about trust…and absolute madness!), any protest my employer might raise will be, as we say, too little too late.

Therefore, allow me to thrust a pinch of frivolity into your soul before you embark upon *And The Rain Continued To Pour*, for goodness knows you're going to need it.

Ahem.

Have you ever noticed how often we say, "Excuse me," or, "Pardon me," to our fellow man? One would think that the situation that calls for such a request would leave the seeker of the pardon in a position of humility, requiring him or her to beseech the offended (however trivial the offense) for said pardon. And yet, after sneezing in another's general direction, or cutting them off as we hoof it to the train, we *command* those we offend to excuse our behavior.

Not only that, but we typically don't wait for a reply, either! We're usually off like a flash before learning whether or not we have been acquitted of the charges. And furthermore, those who should be weighing the transgression on the scales of justice not only fail to do so, but also find the command polite, and thus blithely offer leniency! No investigation, no trial—nothing!

Of course, not everyone fits the mold I have presented. However, those outside the mold are seen as disruptors of society. Imagine a scenario where someone weaving through a crowd bumps your shoulder. Most likely, you, rooted in social convention, would be ready and willing to brush off the offense should the perpetrator turn and offer a casual, "Excuse me." But what if he doesn't? You'd be indignant, no? Now, imagine you are the perpetrator; you bump another person on the shoulder. Per your social training, you call back an, "Excuse me;" but instead of case closed, you are met with a fiery tongue, chastising you for your lack of consideration and audacity to demand pardon!

Both the former and the latter have broken convention, and both are now subject to public ridicule. In the case of the former, that ridicule is warranted. But should the latter be so judged? After all, they were bumped, were they not? And their assailant didn't actually apologize; rather they issued an order to excuse their action, however contrite their inflection might have been.

I say, if we truly seek clemency for our actions, let us invest the proper energy into the obtesting of those we have wounded; and let us, who have been struck by the nasal mist and errant shoulders, be diligent in weighing the malefaction, that we might properly bestow a just verdict upon our wrongdoers!

How was that? Have I successfully injected a little lighthearted-ness into your spirit? Of course, I'm not advocating for people to be overly sensitive. Honestly, I think this world could do with a bit more thick-skinned-ness. So, please, take the above for what it is: a joke; a simple, overly analyzed commentary on a harmless matter. I don't want to see people suddenly taking offense to a rogue sneeze or mild shoulder bump, nor will I accept responsibility for such weak spiritedness.

Moving along!

And The Rain Continued To Pour

ALONG the sidewalk to the crescent, stone steps, situated beside the creek and beneath the shelter, he walked a despondent pace. It was raining even harder now—much harder than it had been when he'd left the house.

On the stone steps he sat, and as the rain continued to soak through his clothes—rendering his expensive ensemble of grey, collared dress shirt, tailored pants, and navy striped tie a sopping mess of fabric—he placed his hand over his mouth in an attempt to prevent that which threatened to make him like the clouds above from escaping his weary heart. But his efforts proved futile, and his tears, refusing to be held captive, began to trickle down his cheek, disguised by the droplets that ran beside them.

Through his enervated, runny eyes, he surveyed the creek as it flowed ever so calmly through the showery scene. Raindrops plunging through the water's surface relentlessly rippled the steady stream and played for him a symphony of splashes. The sound was, to him, reminiscent of a waterfall; and the droning it produced in his ears made him feel as if he were sitting at the base of the cacophonous, though paradoxically peaceful and musical, cascade.

He sat there alone, consumed with sorrow and drenched

with sadness—so weary from an unbridled hoping for what might have been.

He sat there alone, his mind no longer plagued with tormenting thoughts of despair, but slowly settling into silence, becoming cold and numb.

He sat there alone; it was cold, and the rain continued to pour unrelenting down upon him.

He sat there alone until, so unexpectedly, she came to him, breaking through the veil of rain that had him enveloped.

Into his eyes she gazed, just as she had done so many times before, but never like this—this was the first time her eyes had ever beheld him this way, the way he'd ever beheld her since the very first day: passionately, helplessly captivated, and ever so contented.

The world fell silent around them, leaving only the gentle pattering of the rain against their enraptured faces to play in their ears beside the reverberant beating of their hearts and the audible weight of their breath. What was painted upon her face, the need burning in her eyes—these both frightened and delighted him, for his eyes had never before beheld her this way; and he dared to believe that perhaps this mien betrayed that for which he had yearned to find within her since the day he had committed his heart to her.

Slowly she knelt beside him.

He remained frozen, his heart racing: uncertain, but also excited.

And then it happened, so unlike he'd ever imagined it would.

Reaching forth, she tenderly touched the side of his rain-soaked face with her delicate, soft hand, pulled herself slowly toward him; and as time's ticking hands slowed to a halt, she pressed her lips gently and decidedly against his.

There was no more wondering now; there was no question at all.

She had chosen him.

There was no doubt now.

What had forever been a dormant flower began to blossom, as the pair sat atop the crescent, stone steps, sharing in the immeasurable and simple joy of being found within the other's embrace; being held so closely, wrapped in the other's arms, finally and forever.

Had the world ended then and there, it would have made no sound, for nothing—not the world, or any person, place, or problem therein—mattered in that moment.

They had at last found everything, and everything was each other.

The rain continued to pour down upon the pair as they showered one another with their deepest desires, their bodies finally free to hold tight the other, and their hearts finally able to rest in that foreign warmth for which every heart beats to find.

Eternity passed, and a new life was born in the rain that day on the crescent, stone steps beside the creek, beneath the shelter.

His hopeless longing had at last come to an end.

With his trembling hands, he brushed aside the dripping hair that had covered one side of her face, and gently caressed her cheek, all the while lost in her beautiful, blameless eyes.

She was indeed a woman unlike any other, with a smile that

could banish a heart's every shadow, a laugh that eclipsed the song of swaying trees, dancing with a midday, summer breeze; a face like a rare but familiar memory, the kind that seldom breaks through the veil of existence, but leaves for every waking and sleeping moment thereafter a sweet nectar on which to feed; and a soul as pure and untouched as a fresh snow.

There in her eyes he fell deeper and deeper into an enchanted fascination for all that she was; and he felt content to go right on falling and never stop. He could feel her in his arms; he could feel his body pressed against hers; he could feel his heart stop every time their lips met; and he could feel her melting deep into his veins, becoming part of his very being with each passing moment.

The rain continued to pour, and they found themselves somewhere far away from time and space, melding into one.

Taking her hand in his, he, with her, rose from the crescent, stone step, and together they stood amid the downpour.

With his free hand, he grabbed his drenched tie and began loosening it from around his neck. Once undone, he stretched it to full length, and then joined their already united, right hands by a knot tied at the wrist. Having, with her aid, secured the fastening tightly, he extended his untied, left hand to hers in offering.

The drumming of her heart was almost loud enough to hear. Her breaths quivered as they flowed in and out, and her beautiful eyes pierced through the veil of rain, fixing raptly upon his adoring face.

She squeezed tight the hand bound to hers, and then, slowly, as if the motion were a sweet delight of which her gliding fingers desired to savor every taste, she gently placed her free hand in his.

They stood silently for a moment, as the world passed by them in slow motion—a pair of hands bound by his navy striped necktie; the other joined in free will. The energy surging between them was at its highest now, and it peaked as he spoke these words from deep within his heart:

"May the love for which this bond was created never tear apart. May its knot never loosen, and may the hands that complete this bond be ever in free will filled with the one with which it is here joined."

His words were confident, though his body shook violently with what was truly a fearless elation.

"I promise," he said, "that from this moment and into eternity, all that I am and all that I will ever be are yours and yours alone, to have and to hold for as long as I live."

Looking at her and seeing that wonderful, glowing smile, which had parted the clouds of his darkest hour, had caused an obstruction to rise in his throat.

He paused for a moment, as a tear ran the length of his cheek, before continuing.

"You have had my everything," he whispered, "even before this day; and no less will you ever have."

How much more there was he wanted to say; but alas, such words had not yet been invented to offer even an adequate conveyance of his heart's desires.

And, so, he just stood there with his heart in his throat, captivated by every precious detail of the woman he held so dear: the celestial, crystalline shape of her deep, blue eyes; the subtle dimples smiling on her rain-washed cheeks; the way her eyelashes curled like waves on the ocean; the smooth and silky texture of her porcelain skin; and the way in which each individual strand of her coffee-colored hair seemed to radiate its own personal shine—all perfectly portraying, though contradictorily falling short of wholly depicting, the rare beauty she held within. All the world's joy was his and his alone, for he had this woman, this precious woman, and she had him.

There was a time when he used to wonder what she was thinking, what she thought of him whenever he was near, and if she even remembered his face when they were apart. But in that moment, as he held her deep in his arms amid the rain that continued to fall, no such query came to mind, for there existed not a single question regarding her feelings that her eyes or the pressing of her body against his could not answer with absolute clarity. Not a single word or explanation was required.

The future was theirs now. All previous obstacles had been stripped of their power, and the pair was free to live and to love. He knew that this day, like every day he had ever spent with her, would be a day that he would never forget, for the moments that passed were not simply passing moments, but rather lifetimes of inexplicable joy, blessedly shared with the woman whose smile, whose very being, had breathed new life into his soul.

The rain continued to pour relentlessly, but neither he nor she seemed to notice its falling.

His hand caressed the side of her face, and she welcomed his gentle touch, burrowing affectionately into his hand.

He moved his face closer to hers.

Just as their lips were about to touch, he took a deep breath and passionately and powerfully declared for her, as well as words would allow, his every desire, his very purpose, wrapping it all in those three words we know so well.

Their lips finally met in what was the longest and most breathtaking kiss they'd yet shared, one that was thereafter never topped.

And the rain continued to pour down upon him as he sat there alone, his tears disguised by the droplets that ran beside them.

Prologue:
In Darkened Room

BOY, I'll tell you, this has been brutal! I mean where *are* all the uplifting tales, Mr. Conners, *huh*? Three stories in, and not a heartwarming one among them!

I hope you'll pardon my spoiler, dear reader (notice how I didn't *order* you to pardon me). It's not exactly professional of me, I suppose, to reveal that the tale you're about to read is not exactly a jocular, merry one—though if the glaring context clues presented in the title hadn't prepared you for the obvious dispiriting that lies in the offing, I don't know what to tell you. What more could I have done?

I'm beginning to think my boss is a real downer, you know? Perhaps I should have picked up on this by now. After all, I am narrating his novels.

Hmm, I wonder.

I'm sorry, dear reader, but if you could just spare me for a moment, I'd like to mull this over a bit.

I shall be only a minute.

G.O.T.I.T™ *Brain Reader Activated*

Let me see, now. Do those novels contain any—well, there is that one scene where the two guys...yeah, I guess that's a bit unfortunate. Or when they find out that—yup, depressing, for sure. Oh! How about when the girl goes to the place and is—uh huh. Nothing uplifting about that. This shirt is itchy. And then, of course, when that one guy takes the—goodness, how awful! A bit cheesy, perhaps, but still...cheesecake. I could go for some cheesecake, right now. How about the scene where—you know what's better than cheesecake? Deep-dish pizza! Or is it? How about deep-dish AND cheesecake? Trip to the ER, anyone? Oh! I know! That one part I had to write, where the dude from the—nope, just deep-dish. Cheesecake and deep-dish is WAY too much cheese! Darn it. Now I'm hungry. And I can't break away from this narrating until I'm completely done. Is "completely done" redundant? Can you be partially done? People say "completely done" all the time, but now that I think about it, how nonsensical! Done is done, right? No, wait. I think I'm wrong. You can *be partially done. Who invented the business card? But completely done is, actually, redundant. That's like saying done done, which, on a word processor, would produce that little red squiggly line under the second "done." Oh, well; no one will see that after printing. You know, the letter 'x' on my keyboard, like, never gets used—poor little thing. Something should be done about that.*

What was I saying? Is my brain-to-text function running? Oh, no! I think I accidently activated it! How do I turn this thing off? Where's the button? Ah! Found i—

G.O.T.I.T™ *Brain Reader Deactivated*

Forgive my brief absence—I mean, *please* forgive my absence—I mean, *will* you please forgive my absence? Gosh, I really painted myself into a corner there, didn't I?

Okay, back on track.

So, it seems I have inadvertently introduced my G.O.T.I.T. (Gibberish and Other Tumultuous Incoherencies Translator™) system—must have bumped it when I moved away to ponder.

It's a handy little tool, my Brain Reader. It transmits and translates my thoughts into text. There are still a few bugs to work out, but it gets the job done. I don't use it all the time—certainly not when composing a final narrative. It's really for brainstorming only, because, as you witnessed, the brain likes to discuss several topics at once, which makes for a rather literarily cacophonous explosion.

Now, all jokes aside, while it is true that what follows is not a tale filled with the warm fuzzies, its inspiration is no laughing matter.

Though Conners would never classify himself as a poet, he does like to dabble in the discipline every now and then. As a writer, he maintains tremendous confidence in his craft. However, it is a fact widely known by those in his intimate circle that poetry, particularly rhyming poetry, causes him, for whatever reason, to be even more self-critical than usual. Because of this, Conners releases very little poetry to the public, and maintains great respect for those daredevils who publish entire books of poetry.

For Conners, poetry is so very personal that to invite the public to read and critique the quality of what is often a very real representation of his private self would be, in a word, violative. In the case of this next piece, however, because it is of a rare variety of Conners' poetry, which seeks to tell a fantasy in verse, sharing it with the world comes much easier.

In Darkened Room, though a work of fiction, was not without its real-life inspiration. Many years ago, the Author was chatting with a young man who is like a brother to Conners. This young man was, at the time, working as an Emergency Medical Technician, and he told a small but nonetheless captivating tale of an old man he had encountered.

Worn by the years, this elderly gentleman could no longer walk. The young man had been called to his mansion for a routine check, which quickly turned into an emergency hospital visit. Upon returning to the house, he carried the feeble frame of the elderly patient up a giant staircase to his room, where he deposited him, at the old man's request, in a lonely chair, set before a television.

When I asked the Author for more details about this story, he informed me that what else there was to know of the man and his situation was hazy and scarce in the detail department. He said he seemed to remember the young man telling him that the old man just sat perfectly still in the chair, gazing forth with zombie eyes into a static-filled television, which illumed the dark room like a midnight lightning storm. "However," said the Author to me, "that could all have been from my imagination alone."

What he did distinctly remember, though, was the young man's remarks about leaving the room. He said that he was asked by the man to be left alone. He was dismissed, his aid rejected. As he turned to leave, he recalled with gravity the words spoken by the elderly man, imploring him with grave resolution and sadness, that should Death once again come knocking on his door, that he, the young man, would let Death enter, once and for all.

The young man reflected his feelings of sorrow and helplessness, as he backed out of the darkened room and into the hall. He said that as he descended the long staircase, he wondered about the man in a manner that projected the other onto his own self. And as he left the house, before closing the door behind him, he looked one last time to the room he'd left behind, and wished the man peace.

Having heard that story, the Author (as authors tend to do) let his imagination run wild. Feeling great sorrow for the man, Conners set out to capture the essence of our collective fate, and in so doing explore a topic that he believes, due to the immensity of human achievement, is relevant to our time and the future we must all face. To do this, Conners felt it would be best to compose the tale in verse. And he justified this decision, saying, "No one knew his name. His life met a silent end. It had to be sung."

I think that's enough for this little interlude. *In Darkened Room* is next.

Continue!

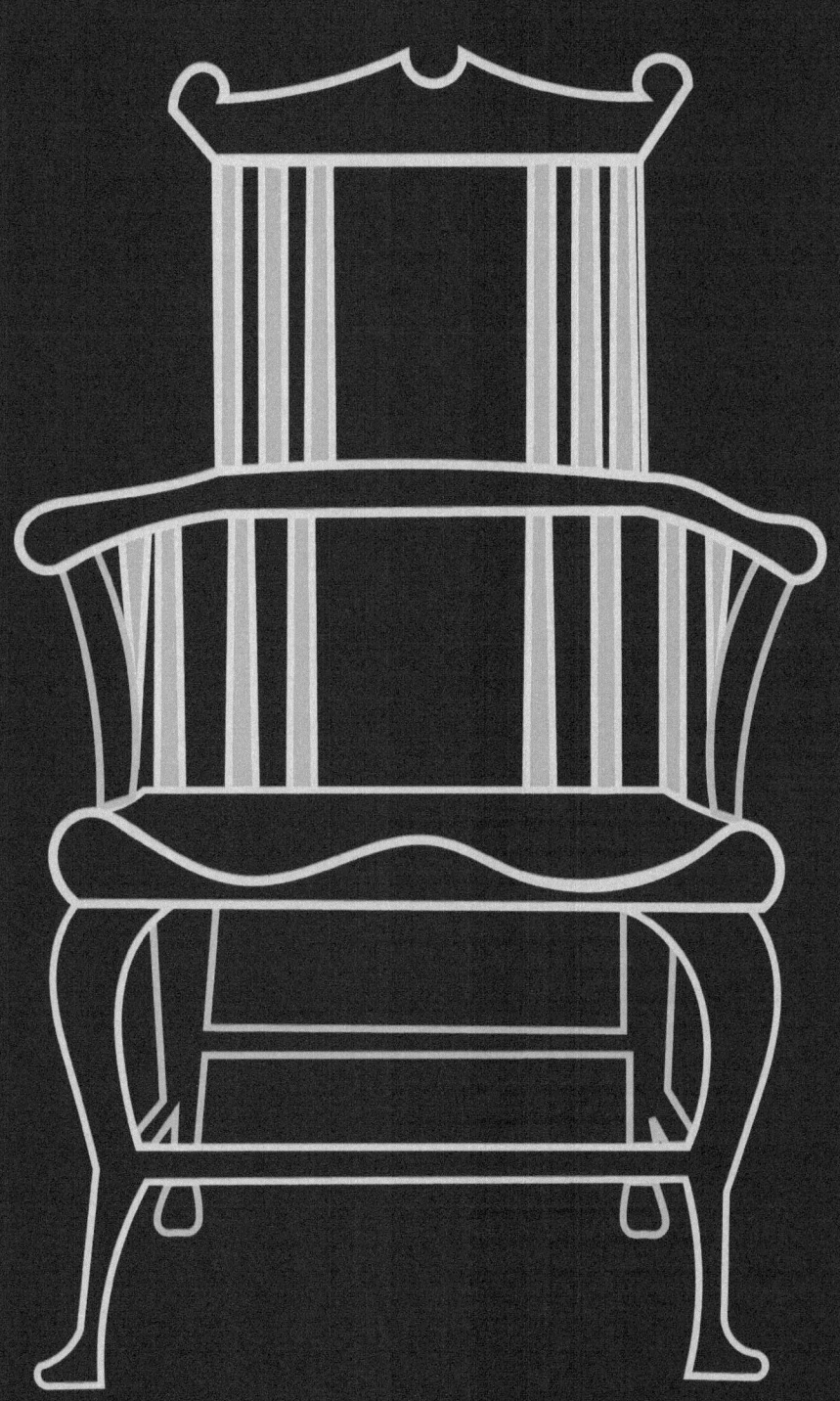

In Darkened Room

"To die, my boy," said he to me,
"There in my chair, just leave me be,
"For I've a weary soul within
"This mangled heap of flesh and sin,
"Which calls me now to take this seat,
"Employ no more these ancient feet."

In room where light's a stranger called,
Up winding stairs, down dreary hall,
Was set a chair, a proud display
Of craftsmanship, like fair array
Made of the finest silk and cloth.
What hands but those so calm and soft
Could forge a piece as this, I thought?
"Come on, now, boy," barked words that fought
'Gainst pondering mind, distracted head,
Which'd left me walking toward the bed
With him who'd long been in my care,
With him these final days'd been shared.

"Not to the bed, thou mindless dunce!
"Take heed my words; listen for once!
"The chair, said I! That wooden seat,
"Whereon a home this rump shall meet."

With haste I wheel'd his body 'round.
Unto the chair our course now bound.
Once there I took his hand in mine
And lifted for the final time
His body frail, weak, and cold.
With tender hands I helped unfold
The limbs that had by years recoil'd,
Like rusted hinges: tight, un-oiled.

A TV screen before him churned
With static flame and light, which burned
A blinding light throughout the room.
Into the screen he stared, consumed.
With what, confess, I cannot say.
'Twas odd to see him stare that way.
But stare he did, his gaze possessed.

"Go on, now, boy. Leave me to rest.
"I'm tired and the end is nigh.
"Trouble not to lift a goodbye.
"Just leave me here to be forgot."

"Forsooth," said I, "I'll surely not!
"Thy life to me is precious still.
"Of life within speak not so ill."

"Enough, dear boy!" his cry rang out,
"And speak no more to me about
"The things thou cannot comprehend.

"'Tis time, my boy. I've reached the end."

"Nay, nay, old man! What speakest thou?"
Declared these lungs with blustery howl.
"Back into life we've rescued thee
"A hundred times! Why, can't you see?
"Thou needst not fear the sting of death,
"For we've the tools to give thee breath,
"Preserve thee here forevermore.
"Repair thy mind, I you implore."

"To thee I said *enough*; now go.
"Content be with mine answer, *no*.
"Machine and man, no kinsmen are.
"In life and death are we apart.
"Unnatural my life of late.
"All eyes within this room berate
"The wretched man set in this chair,
"Who's taken far more than his share.
"For them, time was a frail thing;
"One chance to dance, one song to sing;
"And ne'er to steal another sun,
"Or fight against what life had done
"To skin and soul and youthful grace.
"With courage watched their worlds erased.
"Unhook me, now; remove these wires,
"And let synthetic life expire.
"Leave me to die with these, my friends.
"Leave me to die and make amends

"For all the years that I did hide
"Away from them, the other side."

Then lifted he a shaking hand,
And to the room made last demand.

"Forgive me, friends! Pray mercy show
"This fearful fool, beset with woe!
"Receive me now, if pity be
"Enough to spare the likes of me
"From wandering, as I have, alone!
"No more, dear friends. I'm coming home."

What weight fell on my heart that day
Is still far more than I can say
With any ounce of clarity.
'Twas difficult to hear, for he
Had been my project's volunteer,
A subject I had known for years.
And in that time I'd come to find
A way the Reaper's hands to bind,
And keep the mind from shutting down;
Though for the flesh, no cure's been found.
For forty years did I extend
What nature would have brought to end
The day when on my doorstep he'd
Come crawling on all fours to plead
I spare him his mortality.
With all my heart did I agree.

And for mankind we'd found the way.
With wires and tubes we've let them stay
Here on this earth without an end.
'Tis wonderful to see them spend
A lifetime more than names of old,
Just watching those they used to hold
In youthful arms before they'd grown
To create families of their own.
And watch he did until today
When asked he that I go away,
Unhook from him the life he's known,
And leave him there to die alone.
With broken heart did I obey,
And turned to leave, go on my way,
Abandon all of my success,
And in that room lay him to rest.

Mine eyes surveyed the pictures of
His friends and kin, hung up above.
Content they were; each one at peace.
And from these lungs did I release
A sigh born of my broken heart
For all that'd just been torn apart.
My head hung low, weighed by defeat.
Across the room I slid my feet.
From darkened room, through creaky door,
Down dreary hall to nevermore
Return unto this place of gloom—
A handsome home, fore'er a tomb.

Away from him for good was I,
Parted without a last goodbye.
Then walked I to the pavement's end,
And there with lifted head did send
A steadfast gaze into sky
To watch the earth move slowly by
A world of stars alit with fire,
O'er me, a corpse, riddled with wire.

Prologue:
How I Fell in Love

FINALLY! We have arrived at a story about something happy! I'll bet you thought it would never happen. Believe me, I had my doubts, too.

This one is pretty straightforward, which means I don't think I'll have to spend as much time setting it up, like I have the others.

Praise be! Let us rejoice! The vexatious tongue of the narrator has ceased to prattle!

While I do admire your poised diction, dear reader, I can't say your little outburst doesn't wound me a whit. At any rate, I shall overlook the offense, and continue to "prattle" as if nothing had happened. You and I, as we say in crass terms, are *good*.

How I Fell In Love tells the tale of the pivotal event which led to the engagement of a charming young woman and her fiancé. The strapping lad featured in this piece is a brother-like member of the Author's family; the tale is written from the point of view of this young man's then fiancé and current wife.

The desire to compose this next piece came at a Sicilian summer party, at which time the Author, upon arriving, was reunited with this young man, who then introduced him to his fiancé: a young woman the Author had never met. Though thrilled by the news, the Author, like all who had been blindsided by the bond, could not believe that this young man—who had ever been resolved to live out his life as a hermit in the woods, hunting wild game with his dog, and chasing away anyone who would dare to intrude on his territory—was preparing to settle down with a wife.

Conners, like everyone, though skeptical at first of the sincerity behind the news, believed that such a relationship would convince this man that life in society was not such a bad thing after all. The possibility still looms that there will now be a male and female hermit couple living somewhere in the woods, terrorizing nearby villages, but we're still hopeful. (And if it turns out that he has been right all along about the toxicity of society, then we'll see you in the woods—or we'll see you, but you may not see us…before it's too late).

Having met the darling bride-to-be, Conners and she sat down over pizza and a bowl of spaghetti and meatballs, with a side of garlic bread and a glass of red wine (because what else would Italian-Americans eat at a summer party?), and discussed the particulars of the courtship between her and the six-foot-two giant she'd managed to coil about her little finger. What followed was an absolutely tickling story about how she had fallen in love with him, a story so unique that Conners declared it simply had to be put on paper.

And so was born *How I Fell In Love*: a fictional narrative rooted in one of the more heartwarming and absolutely true tales of young love the Author has ever encountered.

Boom! Under 500 words! Who says I can't exercise brevity every once in a while? Talk about self-control.

Forward!

How I Fell In Love

People often ask, "When did you know?"

I'VE recently become engaged, and every time my fiancé and I stand hand-in-hand before family and friends to give them the exciting news, we, after the hugs, handshakes, and "ball-and-chain" jokes (which never get old), must face the query, "When did you know?"

For the majority of folks with whom we share this news, I know exactly what that question means: "Are you sure you know what you're doing?" would be a more accurate phrasing. You see, my fiancé is not the type of man most would consider the "marrying kind"—especially by his family. If I had a nickel for all the stories to which I've been subjected by his cousins, aunts, uncles, and especially his brothers, regarding all the reasons why this "manly man's man" is the last person on earth anyone would have suspected would take a bride, he and I would be able to pay off this wedding, our student loans, and buy a nice suburban house, with a fence, dog, and snoopy neighbors, and have just enough cash left over for a pizza.

Indeed, he's not your typical Hollywood-type, complete with the tousled, golden locks, chiseled exterior, and elegant attire. He's more the rough-around-the-edges-type, with the jet Mohawk, tattooed arms and chest, and backwoodsman-like frame beneath his holey flannel shirt and tattered jeans: a man who, upon first glance, looks like the type who would have you for dinner should you look at him sideways or have the audacity to offer a cheerful salutation when passing him on the street. But I wouldn't have him any other way, and all those stories they tell me serve only to deepen my love.

But when did it happen? When was the moment? At what point did the stars align and the clouds part, casting forth that angelic light over his broad, boulder shoulders, letting me know that he is the one?

In such cases as these, an audience of excited kith and kin (all working out in their heads the best way to approach the subject of the guest list and wedding party nominees, and subtly submitting their applications for the vacant positions) expect a grand tale, one filled with drama, with broken hearts mended— an enchanting account, fit for the silver screen. Such a story would surely leave the single among them wishing and dreaming for the day his or her own charming someone arrives, and drive the coupled to instantly and internally compare to their own that which might be a more idyllic tale, thus provoking a deep contemplation in which they might generate a few embellishments that will nicely supplement their inferior romantic narrative.

In light of this expectation, I must confess, though not regrettably, that mine is but a simple tale. He and I are no Romeo and Juliet (thank heaven for that; we're both still breathing and not on suicide watch). We are not the fated couple driven apart by circumstance, only to meet again years later, and there in the pouring rain, finally realizing what true love is, embrace and share a passionate kiss. Nor did my fiancé stride in on horseback, slay the dragon, and then rescue me from a tower. Actually, now that I think about it, he did face and succeed in slaying the fiery tongue of my father, and convince him (somehow—I still don't know how) to offer his blessing. That's kind of like slaying a dragon and rescuing me from a tower, I guess.

Any of the latter would be a fancy tale to have under one's belt, but I'm content—thrilled, actually—knowing that mine is simple and unlike any you've probably ever heard.

Allow me to start at the beginning. My fiancé and I met two years ago at a local community baseball game. Though he appeared rather intimidating—what with his tattoos, hulking frame, and coarse hands, as well as that curious scar over his cheek—he was the only man there, including my escort, who, when it was discovered that seating was limited, had the decency to offer me his chair when no one else would. He popped right up, gave me his seat, and proceeded to sit on the grass to continue watching the game.

I did not fall in love with him that day, nor did I have any contact with him for the next few months. Eventually, though, our paths crossed once again. This time I was not accompanied by another man, and was therefore available to open a line of dialogue with the one who would soon steal my heart. What I discovered over the course of the next few months was a man who, though true to his powerful façade, had a beautifully gentle spirit. I won't go into detail, for such things are for him and me to share. In addition, though I doubt any of his friends are readers, should any of his buddies discover his sweeter side, they would undoubtedly submit him to torment (and I fear for *their* wellbeing, not my beloved's, of course).

Still, even after all that time spent getting to know him better, I cannot say I was really in love. He and I were close; there's no doubt about that. But Cupid had not yet fired his arrow—though I know he had already taken aim.

One evening, my soon-to-be-fiancé and I were camped along a quiet lake. Having spent all day fishing—an endeavor which saw him bring home enough trout to feed a family of twelve, and me reel in a log and an impressive assortment of refuse—we found ourselves a bit sleepy. We were just sitting with our toes in the sand, watching the western sky become alit with flame, and listening to the soothing buzz of the wild life. Because of my drowsy state, I cannot recall what exactly had sparked us to do so, but we soon found ourselves, as young couples often do, rolling about the sand. He was playfully wrestling me into a giant bear hug and tickling the wind from my lungs.

In his giant arms, my back to his chest, I struggled gleefully but in vain, until, in a moment I shall never forget, my hand came to rest in his. The tickling stopped, and we both paused. As the weight of the first time our hands had joined sank in, I felt something I'd never before felt.

Was it love? Well, no, not yet. It was actually a foreign sense of security. I felt, to put it simply, safe. And that, coupled with the fact that I'd just been tickled half to death after an exhausting day of log and garbage fishing, caused me, instantly and involuntarily, to drop my head into my chest and (I kid you not) fall fast asleep.

He held me as I slept, though I cannot say exactly how long that was. It was extremely pleasant, though—and maybe a bit embarrassing, now that I think about it. But was it the security and pleasant slumber that had caused me to fall in love, to know that this was the man with whom I was destined to share my life?

Nope.

It was what happened just after that.

My eyes fluttered awake to the sensation of something cool, soft, and a bit tickling atop my cheek. He and I had not yet shared a first kiss. Could this be that euphoric moment, I wondered? Might this towering, burly, teddy-bear-slash-walking-Humvee of a man be so wonderfully pressing his lips onto my cheek, for the very first time?

Words cannot express the elation I felt as I turned my waking eyes toward him, hoping to find his face, and there share a first, non-cheek kiss.

But I didn't find his face.

There were no lips upon my cheek; nothing of him at all… except the spider he'd placed there.

And that's when I knew.

Prologue: Lady

AND we're back to business as usual. Hope you enjoyed your moment of uplift, because this next piece is gonna bring you—
 Wait a second.
Which piece is this?
Let me check my notes, here, for a moment.
Oh! *This* one!

Well, you can forget what I was saying, dear reader. I was under the impression that the Author was running with a different set of stories, an original list that has since been amended. The piece I had thought was next in sequence was omitted at the last minute and replaced with the forthcoming *Lady*.

I remember the conversation distinctly—it's all coming back to me, now. Upon presenting me with the original list of stories for this compilation, the Author, who had just finished proofreading each, and had entered my office wearing a lugubrious mien (eyes distant, gazing gloomily atop two large, dark bean bags; lips pale and drooping like branches on a willow tree, producing low, dismal sounds; shoulders dropped and arms swinging heavily), turned without a word and shuffled slowly into the hall. Obviously concerned, I finished my morning coffee and eggs, watched the remainder of the television show episode playing on my laptop, and then hurried off to find my boss.

You may criticize my decision to savor every last bite of my breakfast and absorb every last laugh from one of my favorite shows, instead of rushing out immediately at the first sign of trouble. But, in my defense, it is a proven fact (either by science or out of the necessity to fortify this argument) that a man with an empty stomach and unalleviated stress, not to mention an incomplete daily dose of his favorite stimulant, is less than useless in a situation requiring his unmitigated attention.

They (whomever those ambiguous experts are that everyone regularly quotes) say that when endeavoring to rescue someone who is drowning, one should remember first not to put one's self at risk, as such does nothing to aid the one in need. Thus was my reasoning in this scenario. Had my brain not been completely enlivened by the morning tonic, fed by the debated first or second comer of nature's most delicious and common-flavored creature, and eased into a state of clarity by some truly diverting cinematic material, any assistance I might have provided my employer could have been detrimental to the preservation of both our lives.

I think that's justification enough.

Anyway, I found him sitting in the kitchen, his head buried in (I kid you not) a birthday cake.

This is not a figure of speech—his head was literally submerged in a cake.

Though alarmed by the sight, I was not concerned for his safety, for the oddest element of this scene had caught my eye the second I had entered the room: a snorkel.

Yes, the Author was snorkeling inside of a traditional, white frosting, six-inch high, circular birthday cake.

Why?

Oh, believe me, I asked him why.

Narrator: "What are you doing?"

Narrator retrieves head of his employer from pastry.

Author: "Hello?"

Narrator: "I said what are you doing?"

Author stares with mouth gaping; eyes clogged with cake and frosting.

Author: "I felt like snorkeling."

Narrator: "What for?"

Author: "'For what reason' would be a more acceptable, grammatical manner in which to structure your query."

Narrator, still holding Author's head by neck, contemplates tossing said head back into sea of mangled pastry. Speaks with clenched teeth.

Narrator: "Why are you snorkeling inside a cake?"

Author: "I felt it might serve to ease my mind."

Narrator: "Are you feeling uneasy?"

Author: "You always were quite adept at unearthing the obvious."

Narrator considers hitting Author with brick.

Narrator: "Why are you uneasy?"

Author: "I've spent the last six days reviewing a series of somber stories. Today I was struck by the realization that my life was lacking in sweetness. Thus I plunged—"

Narrator: "—Into a cake."

Author: "Precisely."

Narrator: "You ought to be committed, you know that?"

Author: "I would be if any woman would have me."

Narrator experiences violent twitch.

Narrator: "No, I meant you're crazy."

Author: "Sane is merely another word for 'uninspired.'"

Narrator drops Author's head, which lands heavily into cake with loud thud that echoes through room.

Author: "Prmhmphs mmhph shurmpd—"

Narrator lifts Author's head from within cake.

Narrator: "What was that?"

Author gasps, then licks lips.

Author: "Perhaps I should revise my story list—insert a few cheerier pieces."

Narrator: "I think that's a fine idea."

Author: "Yes. I'll see if I can find anything merrier, perhaps hidden somewhere—like here, for instance, in Suzie Shortening's

De-lish Locker."

Narrator: "You do that."

Narrator drops Author's head, which crashes into cake with loud thud.

Narrator: "Let me know when you find something. I'll be in my office."

In case you were wondering, Mr. Conners is quite all right, now. He hasn't snorkeled inside a cake, or any pastry of which I am aware, since that day. I will not go so far as to say he is completely sane, for to do so would be to deny my conscience and reject logic. And while I know it is true that some of the oddest among men have gone on to be revered as great artists, innovators, intellectuals, etcetera, I am doubtful my employer can be considered a peer among such a distinguished, significant group as that. He may just be plain old nuts.

Anyway, what were we talking about? (Or, *About what were we talking?* to appease the grammaticist that is my employer, who obviously doesn't subscribe to the Winston Churchill position on ending sentences with propositions…and who, I fear, may be rubbing off on me).

Right! *Lady*!

This one is rather straightforward. The idea for *Lady* came to the Author one day whilst napping in the mid-afternoon. A vision of the climatic scene you are about to read leapt into his sleeping mind, painting in vivid detail the events of what would become the fifth installment of this compilation. Because dreams tend to be like those self-destructing mission briefing tapes sent to secret agents, the Author sprang from his bed—eyes still rolling about their sockets, and appendages still detached from the body—and began typing furiously on his laptop.

Roughly thirty minutes later, Conners regained consciousness, and there on his computer screen beheld a first and final draft of a brand new story. It is often the case with the Author, as well as many artists of various crafts, that the process of composing an artistic piece is in no small way a subconscious, out-of-body experience, wherein one feels as they go along like they are discovering the piece. The Author has sometimes described this experience as peeling away the white strips of the page that cover the words of a story already written there.

What was born that day, transferred from a dream to the blank spaces of the page, is a tale of woe, of warning, which bears a message of hope and inspiration. *Lady* tells the story of a life changed in the blink of an eye, and that life's passionate struggle to reclaim what was through laxity and ignorance lost.

And so, let us move along from this borderline interminable intermission, and experience the rousing tale, *Lady*.

Carry on! (Or, *"Carry thyself onward!"*).

Lady

A blink of an eye—that's all it took.

***

SHE was indeed lovely, my precious lady. How high above me she was—towering; so colossal in constitution and vast in worth, she was almost too beautiful to be fathomed. She was mine; a perfect fit. And yet, though I knew she was there, I rarely ever saw her. It was as if—no, it was *exactly* that I, basically, became used to her being around. We'd been together since my youth, so long that our relationship was more a given, and less something on which I needed to work, on which I needed to invest my time and energy.

Whenever people would ask me about her, my response was always the same. "She's a sweet ol' gal," I would say, or, "She's sure good to me," or, "Of course I know I'm blessed to have her." The latter usually came when others would remind me that not everyone had a lady so sweet of whom to boast.

I wouldn't say it was irritating to hear so many people remind me of how lucky and blessed I was to have her, nor did the hatred received from others, who knew not my lady's blessings and comforts, affect me in the slightest. They could scream all they wanted, as far as I was concerned—scratch us with their claws; my lady wasn't going anywhere. She'd been through a great deal in her day; she could handle it.

I could never remember more than the basics of her history, for it had been my belief that understanding the particulars was not only boring and tedious, but also rather irrelevant. The way I looked at it, why should I waste my time learning the places whence she'd come? Sure, they made her who she was, but was that relevant to the now? I thought not. Actually, I never thought about it at all. I had the present product; and with that, even ignorant of it most of the time, I was content.

And then times got hard; there were always tough times. We'd had our share of ups and downs. There were even years when, I'll admit, I'd felt like the ship was going to capsize. But the waters would always level out in the end, allowing me to go right back to basking in the warmth of her embrace.

By heaven's design was she formed; by its light did she walk, and I with her, hand in hand, across vast deserts and fruitful plains, over cathedral mountains, and across mighty seas, all the way singing a love song I had long ago written about and for her. The warmth of heaven was in her touch, and though my eyes seldom lifted to the light by which we walked, its warmth was ever upon me.

She was good to me, my lady. She was very good to me. Even though I seemed to notice her only when the sky appeared to be falling, she was good to me. But this hard time, this particular patch of rocky waters—for this I was not ready.

***

The words are clear. They are of my tongue—my dialect, even. There is no mistaking so much as a syllable pouring forth into my ears. And there had better be no mistaking. Such has proven fatal. If there is a mercy to be found, a silver lining, if you will, it is that every syllable is piercingly loud, painful sometimes. Yes, the volume helps to ensure that there is no mistaking what is being said. But as every syllable burrows into my skin and rattles my bones I become more and more aware of reality; I become increasingly gripped by fear, fear so paralyzing that I fear the fear will buckle my legs, ushering forth that in which my every fear is rooted.

I know what I must do, what is expected of me, of us; and I do it without hesitation.

I do not wait.

I do not think.

I do not protest.

I obey.

***

Did my sweet lady leave me, or was she taken away? Or did I give her away? Did I simply let her go?

These questions I have pondered tirelessly, anxiously, miserably, over and over since the day the rocks were allowed to overset the ship of our union.

I never saw those rocks.

That's a lie.

I saw them.

I saw them every day.

I just never really looked at them.

Sometimes they would scrape the sides of the vessel;

occasionally we would bounce off of one; but most of the time they seemed more like gnats or mosquitoes on a hot, summer day: pests, annoyances—mostly harmless, just nettlesome and disruptive of one's peace. The remedy, I'd found, was not to grab hold of the helm and steer my lady and me out of the perilous waters into which we'd sailed, but instead to sink further and further below deck, deeper into corners and beneath blankets, and there fix my eyes upon a distraction, place my fingers into my ears, hum that old love song, while my lady sat alone somewhere above deck.

Ignorance sailed the ship. Not particularly well, of course, but well enough, I'd thought.

I had truly believed this union of ours was indestructible. I had truly believed that no matter what rocks came into our path, no matter how turbulent the seas became, she would somehow pull us through like she had always done, and I with her would enjoy the fruits of smooth sailing. I never knew, or perhaps I'd just forgotten, that she had needed me just as much as I had needed her. Or maybe it was I alone who had needed her. Maybe she wasn't the type who had ever needed anybody, but was instead the type who goes only where she is wanted, whose blessings are reserved only for those who truly want her around, those who are willing to invest in her, pay attention to her, to fight for her—those who are unlike me.

Goodness knows I'm not the person I once was.

***

Line by line; row on row—this seems to be the new norm. It is here, in this place, stripped of my identity, that I realize just how many were like me, how many weren't good to their sweet lady. I realize that I am not the protagonist; I am the chorus. And how silent have I been. How silent have we all been.

My sweet lady—she was mine alone. And yet, in the same way, she was ours. But she did not belong to us; we belonged to her. And instead of reminding her that such was our desire, we'd demonstrated in word and in deed, and in the dearth of word and deed, how much we desired her absence. Again and again we begged—idly we begged, not knowing what we were saying, for we knew not our beloved—to be released from her embrace, to be cast into the night, to see her no more that we might know the mighty clutches of him we knew not, but sorely deserved. Never would we, with forthright tongues, have asked for his ensnaring embrace. And yet we did, forthrightly, with all that our afeared tongues did not say, with all that our ignorant lips spouted, with all the fury of our stubbornly marching feet, and with all the stillness of our atrophied legs.

He is ever-present, just as she was.

But we'd never noticed her.

We notice him, for sure.

***

The morning when she left was not a silent dawn. Roused from my bed by the blaring of mighty trumpets, the kind that sound from far beyond the atmosphere and shake the skeletal frame near to shattering, I soon found myself in the arms of those I'd once believed were my kinsmen, my brethren, my friends. But they were so cold, so distant. They were not the family I thought I'd known.

She had left without a sound. Actually, now that I think about it, there was plenty of sound. It was triumphant. It was joyous. It was jubilant and gay. It was fantastic, just fantastic, and unlike anything I'd ever heard. But the sound did not sing of her departure—no. In fact, the sound was, in a way, intended to have been a celebration *of* her—at least, that's how I had intended.

Looking back, I see just how far from the essence of her heart that celebration had been. I guess I'd thought she would have been pleased, that it was something of which she'd approve. I was doing it for us, for her and me, for our future—or, to be real, I was just sitting back and watching everyone else, those who presently stare at me coldly, as they set the wheels of our future in motion.

Did I understand it? No. Not one bit. But she did. She must have. For the next day she was gone. In the blink of an eye she was gone. And I never knew her better or missed her more than on that day.

***

Everyone is still. We must all face forward. I have lost all track of time since this new chapter began, since I was from my warm bed taken by those whom I'd been told were my friends, and placed inside this massive grave.

All of us, thousands upon thousands, stand barefoot amid the frigid, winter air. There are hundreds of millions like us. We are but one organized group of a thousand, guarded by the few, ordered together by some code or formula created and set in place by those who have become our owners: those for whom we'd willingly paid.

Our rags, the ones attempting to cover our quivering legs and quaking torsos, were forged from the molested remains of the grand and beautiful garment our sweet lady had once knitted for and wrapped about us, the one that had by the blood of our hands and the sweat of our brows, long ago, when we were so young, been painted.

We wear it, now, in shame.

Holey messes, they are: burned, frayed, shredded. We wear them that our masters might mock us. They believe it humorous to see their slaves donning what could have been an imperishable garment, had we but cared for it: carefully washing them rather than spitting on them to make them clean; sewing back loose threads, instead of pulling and pulling and pulling on them, unraveling entire sections. They laugh as their own knitted design—a perverted rearranging of our own, the one this false kindred of the few once claimed to love—flies proudly overhead and on their breasts.

They find our attire, our humility very funny, indeed.

I find it fitting…regrettably fitting.

***

Oh, sweet lady—where art thou! To thee I plead! Return unto me; oh, return unto me, dearest lady, that I might prove unto you the full measure of my devotion, which has ne'er stronger been, nor less shall it ever be! Ardently will it grow, forevermore!

Return to me, dear lady! Let me feel the warmth of heaven in your hand, that precious hand this fool had spurned for the chill of his own! Let me look upon the light that had you formed and our paths made right! Deliver me, as you once did, from this bondage, foisted ignorantly, though nonetheless willingly, upon my despicable self!

Deliver me, and I shall ever be thy champion!

***

It is silent; thusly did our orders command.

We stand—thousands upon thousands with helpless, defeated heads bowed—before our masters: the few, the powerful. They watch us with unwavering eyes; they know us through and through; oh, how well they know our hearts!

Foolish were we to invite them; foolish were we to give them our trust, our hope, our strength. We have nothing—only the cold, blistering air and the snow at our feet, amid the dusty ground within the barbed wire fortress, where now we live. And here shall we ever—

"SILENCE!"

What was that? My head snaps to the right. I dare not lift it, for it must remain bowed, per my master's orders; but I cannot resist this impulse to look toward the sound.

It was a master who had yelled. He seems to have taken issue with one of my fellow slaves.

But why? Given the master's cry, he must have broken silence.

But how? What did my kinsman say?

A cold, eerie stillness fills the frigid scene as I watch the master march toward someone in a line not far from my own. Is it a he or a she? I cannot tell. That head is as bare as mine, and none of us has enough life in our veins to expose our individuality. The master stares menacingly into my kinsman's eyes; my kinsman's head remains lowered. The other masters are screaming at the rest of us to return our eyes to the ground, to disregard that which is taking place at the other end of the line.

But I cannot refrain.

I must look.

My kinsman, head bowed, stares into the ground, appearing defeated.

What had they said, I wonder?

I suppose I'll never—

Wait! My kinsman now lifts his or her head to the master, locking eyes with him, defiantly. The turning of the earth slows, and I see my kinsman's lips separate.

They are moving to speak.

BANG!

Before a sound can be lifted, before an eye can blink, my kinsman collapses lifelessly to the ground: a bloody heap upon the frozen earth. The master, having spat upon the corpse, now turns away and replaces himself in the foreground.

All heads have fallen back into place.

No one looks up.

All are shaking, both from the cold and from the—

What's that? Another voice? Another kinsman breaking silence?
It can't be.

"SILENCE!"

The voice of the master roars through the wide space, as an
inaudible gasp surges through the lines. This sound of my kinsman's disobedience rose from my left. I turn my head slightly; I
cannot see…but now I can clearly hear.

It is the love song, our love song, my lady's and mine; the one
we all used to sing at the sight of our beloved departed and the
rags we now wear, when into the sky were they hoisted, whole,
free, and powerful. My kinsman is singing—they're singing our
song! And now I can hear what it was the other, now dead, had
said. He'd raised his or her voice, all alone, lifting the first line of
our dear song into the frigid air. And he or she was butchered
for it.

"SILENCE!"

A master on the left storms from her position in the foreground
toward my singing kinsman. This time there is no hesitation.

BANG!

I hear a crumbling thud. My eyes squeeze tightly and my

stomach begins to climb my esophagus, readying to empty its barren contents. This nightmare is—

"SILENCE!"

Another voice rings out, loud and clear, singing from the very spot our fallen kinsman had by the roar of thunder been cut down, but not silenced—that voice lives on, undefeated!

BANG!

There is no pause following this clamor of death—another voice from another direction takes up the mantle and begins singing the very next note. Another voice joins in unison. The harmony sounds like the inception of flight feels.

BANG!
BANG!

I can hear no crumpling of bodies.

BANG!

No cries of pain.

BANG!

The air is filled only with singing! So many are singing, now! Whether these voices ever knew or meant these words when before they sang as free men and women, they know and mean them today. They sing unabashedly, undauntedly, unaware of the bloodstained faces with snarling lips and knitted brows weaving through the lines with smoking hands.

BANG!
BANG!
BANG!

Never have I heard voices so sweet; goose bumps erupt all over me.

BANG!

A fire begins to burn within me.

BANG!

Tears form behind my eyes.

BANG!
BANG!

I become inflated with courage, with desire, with rage.

BANG!

I am not afraid.

BANG!

And so, as blood flies through the air, painting red the passing, biting snow, as well as my tearstained face…

BANG!
BANG!

…I close tight my eyes—shots ringing out in all directions, but becoming increasingly muted as the chorus unties—and raise my head and arms to the heavens. And with the mighty chorus, now arrived at the crescendo, and with the ireful presence of black eyes bearing down upon me, I open my lungs and sing that final, beautiful verse!

BANG!

***

She was my lady, and she was indeed lovely. But I never truly saw her, not until today. In the blink of an eye she was gone. In the blink of an eye all that I had ever known had disappeared.

And there was no one but me to blame.

***

A blink of an eye—that's all it took.

In the blink of an eye I'd lost everything, and in the blink of an eye was everything reclaimed. My sweet lady; she returned to me. She delivered me from bondage. She was alive in me all along, and now she is alive in the many.

From my place upon the frozen earth I watch as thousands upon thousands of my kindred rush their masters. We sang a joyous hymn, one we all know well, but never really knew until today. Our masters have expired their weapons and flee now in terror, as the ones their numbers few had long controlled take up the arms that had once held them in submission, and charge with reclamation and reformation on their minds, and perfervid ire and righteous indignation in their hearts. They rush past my bloodied, broken body, screaming my dear, sweet lady's name as they go.

My heart is weakening, and yet I feel stronger than ever. A tear falls from my eye and into the pool of my blood. I do so wish I could join them. But my part has been played. The curtain moves now to close. And, once again, for the last time, here, I will close tight these weary eyes. What awaits them when again they open? I can only hope, but I cannot tell.

For in the blink of an eye, so much can change.

Prologue:
Snowfall

HAVE you, dear reader, ever seen a movie that features a scene that's either so redundant, irrelevant, or so obviously out of place that you wonder if it had been inserted solely to pad the runtime? Well, that's *certainly* not what's happening with this next story.

Snowfall was handpicked from a vast assortment of worthy stories, because the Author and I agreed that it provided another face of the multifaceted visage that is the work and complexion of C. K. Conners, while also contributing a sort of balance to what might otherwise have been a purely somber collection. I can assure you it was not selected in desperation from a pile of old, disregarded pieces, because the piece the Author had originally intended to include featured a celebrity as a character, which, as was discovered last minute, can get one into serious legal trouble; and since neither the Author nor I have anything but moths boring holes in our pockets (moths who are also dead broke, by the way), and would therefore be plumb ruined should that celebrity take action, that hilarious and pleasantly diverting story regrettably had to be pulled, leaving a gap in need of filling, the remedy for which was a long forgotten story from February (make sure you acknowledge the 'r') of 2012, which the Author, in an hour (literally the hour before the present one), dissected, revised, renamed, and spat into this collection—*safe*!

Pauses for necessary post-run-on-sentence breather

So, yeah. That's totally not what's going on here.

All right, you want the real story?

Fine. Here it goes.

Originally, Mr. Conners had wanted to feature one of his more humorous stories in this collection; however, as stated prior, the fact that one of the characters was a celebrity—albeit a clone of that celebrity—he and I deemed it wiser not to tempt said celebrity's lawyers. While we do think that celebrity would appreciate the story, it really would be unfair to make money off of their likeness without permission.

The ideal number for this compilation was seven; so, the Author began poring through some old work. Because he has spent so much of his recent energy in writing his novels, there really weren't many from which to choose. Some of the standouts considered were a set of letters to an old friend, one of which was never sent; a story written for a Biology class, and a very short, largely forgotten tale, composed on a frigid, winter's night.

The first of these, one of the two letters, detailed a hypothetical idea, in which, as I understand it, the Author discovers some sort of life meaning while talking to a wall—I *think* that's how it goes. The second, unsent letter, written many years ago, performs and presents a detailed analysis of the male and female psyches, and, using a diagnosis of common relationship motifs, explores how they complement and repel one another, before submitting several theories for some presently unexplained phenomena inherent to the inner workings of both sexes, while also concocting metaphorical scenarios to illustrate several unspoken relationship laws.

He was a teenager when he wrote that piece—and he had intended to send it as a letter to a friend.

What a weirdo.

Another standout was a piece written for a college Biology class. He'd written two notable pieces for this class; however, since one had been published by the college, only the other was eligible to be published here. The available piece explained eukaryote cells as if their components were members of a community. While the personification of these components had been the professor's idea and assignment, Conners composed his piece in verse from the point of view of a tour guide, making a rather lighthearted, children's-story-like, educational piece that just didn't make the cut for this compilation, but may yet meet the public eye.

In the end, however, a small, very short story, originally called *The Snowfall*, won the coveted sixth spot in this seven-story book.

Written in early 2012, the recently revised *Snowfall* takes us into a very real, though slightly embellished, night had by the Author. There are no fairies or goblins, or princesses locked in far away towers—nothing of that variety of extraordinary. However, what was extraordinary was the simple, yet personally profound meaning the Author took away from a midnight walk through a midnight snowfall.

You, dear reader, may find what follows this intermission trivial, unworthy of a second read, completely unremarkable. But you may find, as the Author did, something quite special. You may find, as you read, that in what is common, in what is obvious, lies something that, though known to be present, needs only to be seen once again in order to realize potential and make a truly inspiring change.

I give you *Snowfall.*

Advance!

Snowfall

THE hour was late, the sky was dark, and the world was already fast asleep. Having completed my work, I made my way ever so silently through empty rooms, extinguishing any light still burning.

The house now cloaked in midnight, I moseyed blindly along black hallways to the stairs leading up to my room. But as my foot touched down upon the first step, I noticed through a window to my right a lonely streetlamp keeping its empty corner of the road awake. What I could not see in darkness was illumed beneath the lamp's beam: a gentle snowfall.

Being as I am of the limited variety of humans inhabiting this earth who find snowdrifts and nasal icicles more appealing than sand dunes and suntans, my heart leapt inside my chest, completing an impressive triple backflip and sticking the landing perfectly.

Every year since I was a boy I have prayed for subzero temperatures and devastating blizzards; so, whenever I see a light drizzling of snow outside my door, I instantly become ten years old again, and am compelled to lace up the boots, jump into the snow pants, and go frolicking about until the pneumonia takes hold.

I ran for the door.

Stepping out into the breathtaking, glorious cold, I stood among millions upon millions of tiny, falling specks of lace, which danced gracefully and independently on the steady breeze before settling atop one another in their temporary, earthly abode. My enraptured body, so caught up in the magnificence and splendor of the moment, warmly welcomed the nipping chill, finding its sting most electrifying.

Everything was so clear, so peaceful, so silent: a trademark of the season. Never have I stood among the heavenly, silken diamonds and heard anything but the powerful silence, the all-consuming peace that comes from the spell of tranquility and the hushed lullaby of a descending wonderland. The world is a noisy place, filled to the brim with cacophonous sounds that ripple through its inhabitants, straining and numbing the nerves in such a subtle way that we who dwell among the tumult never quite realize the full extent of the harassment our souls have endured. It is only on nights such as these that we—if we allow ourselves to be still—may come to realize the truth of our unknown plight; for when the snow falls, all the world stops to listen.

I was alive. Life itself had never been so vivid in me. Well, maybe it had. Perhaps I'd just forgotten. The life I found within me that night was not foreign—no, it felt like a memory, like something I'd long ago held dear, something on which time had caused me to loosen my grip. If I could only remember what exactly that life had been. More than that, who had *I* been?

Confused but exhilarated, I closed my eyes and fantasized that I had fallen into the passing breeze and was being carried away on the wings of the wind, dancing freely with the snow as I went. But as I danced I wept for the life I could not remember, and my heart sang a lament for the warmth it had forgotten. Suspended in air, my arms ached to embrace every piece of heaven falling beside and all around me, and my hands wished to become one with the earth, that they might hold for a time what would be but a fleeting visitor.

As the breeze slowed into stillness, I beat the air with my arms, fighting to maintain my place in the sky. But it was no use. Exhausted, my body drifted gently to the ground; and there, lying on my back, I watched the snow descend upon me.

Eyeing each flake with passionate intensity, I soon took note of their complex compositions. Each was obviously unique; however, what took my eye was not the fact that each bore a design all its own, but rather a piece of the life I'd forgotten. They were small, fleeting visions, these fragments; and they passed so quickly that I began to beg each individual flake to remain suspended for just a moment or two longer, that I might remake a faded memory.

But they refused to halt.

I wanted more. I *needed* more. This life I once knew, whatever it had been—I needed it so badly, though I knew not why. Those fading pictures both delighted and haunted me, for in them I saw everything—everything I desperately wanted to recapture and everything I desperately wanted to forget.

I drifted to sleep atop the frozen earth, but I was ever conscious of the snowflakes. Anxiously, in a dream, I tried frantically to absorb through my pores that old life, and I raced wildly through the corners of my mind, searching for any glimpses or photographs that might help me recapture what had been lost.

But I found nothing.

That life was gone.

As would the snow falling from the night sky, it had lingered but a short time. All that remained were flashes of incomplete memories, made in the moments before my slumber.

I awoke the next morning in bed. How I'd gotten there, I cannot say. Rubbing the sleep out of my eyes, I shuffled dazedly to my window. There below was my world, painted a pristine white. Trees were draped with glistening linens, and the ground was a soft, clean bed, completely undisturbed. As I admired the beauty of the scene that lay before me, I was reminded that my life, my world, could still be a blank canvas. My story had not yet been written in full—there was still time to take what had been etched upon my history and make things new again. The memories of the life I'd left behind, which had been sprinkled over me the night before, and which rested now outside my window— they would always be there to guide my hand as it composed a new narrative, painted a new beginning, and told a new story.

But where to begin?

Having dressed quickly, I flung open the door, took in a long, deep breath of the fresh air, and then scampered off to build a snowman.

Prologue:
The Candidate

YOU know what's awful, my dear reader?

Job Hunting.

The Author and I have held a variety of odd jobs, some worth more storytelling material than others. However, what we both found upon concluding our collegiate careers was a world of closed doors.

I, like the Author, have worked since I was sixteen, and during college I worked full-time to pay for tuition and avoid loans. However, even after all those years spent accumulating experience in the "real world," and with what I'd been told was the magical bachelor's degree earned from an accredited university under my belt, I found, as many have, that starting a career was not as easy as I'd been led to believe. Even with the degree, which stated that I had been educated in a highly desirable field, I could not land a low-paying, entry-level job that would, as I'd hoped, enhance my skills and provide me with the experience I would need to climb the ladder. Why? Because every place to which I applied required at least two to three years of relevant experience!

Wait, what? You're telling me that in order to get the experience I need to start a career, I need experience? How does that work?

It's similar to the time I'd applied for a credit card. Because I'd wanted to establish a credit history that might one day assist in my purchasing of a home, I applied for a basic card, but was rejected because, get this, I HAD NO CREDIT HISTORY!

Seriously? That's the whole reason I'd applied in the first place!

If you're on the hunt for a job, dear reader, or about to commence your search, take this qualified advice: get an internship, volunteer, network like crazy, and approach every job with the mindset that you will one day rule the company.

And from whom, I can hear you ask, *cometh this, as thou sayest, "qualified" advice? Certainty not thee, for 'twould seem, based upon thy failures in* le markét de jobs*, that such advice has by you been effectuated not, thus providing thee no evidence that such advice would further mine own pursuit. Else thou art merely repackaging a formula that has for thee proven ineffective, believing it might for another produce propitious results—a doltish effort, but one I might have from thee expected.*

What a gem you are! What a rare and charming tongue you possess! I do indeed enjoy your colorful barbs, every now and then.

Anyway, no, you are correct; this advice comes not from me, but rather from a man to whom you shall soon be introduced: a man known as *The Candidate*. (How about that for a segue, huh?)

Yes, dear reader, we have reached the final installment of this seven-story collection. Hold onto your hat (or toupee, or whatever might by breaking, literary force be jettisoned from your head); this one is a doozy. And I mean that. Be warned, dear reader, this story contains potentially disturbing content.

The longest by far in this compilation, making up more than half of this book's total word count, *The Candidate* tells the tale of a young man who is hired as a management intern for one of the biggest and most prestigious companies in the world. His boss—a distant, uninterested, walking metaphor—wants nothing more than to pass off the running of his company to his intern staff that he might bask in the spoils of his empire. What follows is a cautionary tale, demonstrating the destructive path a set of good intentions mixed with ruthless ambition can forge when paired with a dominant power, rife with indifference and ignorance.

Chapter One of *The Candidate* was initially featured as a blog post on CKConners.com, published in August 2015. Though it was praised by some, not another word of the story was ever published. Why? Because nothing else had been written! Conners had shelved the project indefinitely in order to complete his first novel; and he did not pick up the pen again until exactly one year after Chapter One's release, at which time planning had begun for *The Ramblings of a Small-Town What's-His-Name*.

Seeing an opportunity to revisit the world of *The Candidate*, Mr. Conners dove headlong into its development, forsaking all other projects, and completed the five-chapter story in a fortnight…which may sound moderately impressive until you learn that, over a year later, the story underwent a massive rewrite: an episode from which the forcibly evicted hairs upon the Author's head have yet to see newcomers occupy their vacant spaces.

"I'd waited far too long to finish this story," he said to me upon wrapping the final chapter, while also taping gobs of darkly-painted grass clippings to his bald spots. "Many times it seemed *The Candidate*'s day would never come; but the timing could not have been better."

And I quite agree.

Ladies and gentlemen, meet *The Candidate*.

Onward!

The Candidate
Chapter I
The Interview

When did it happen? Oh, I *vividly remember the day. Long have I relived it, over and over in my mind; so clear has that day become that whenever I venture into that dark corner of my mind, I nearly literally take a step back in time. I lie here and ponder, simmer, and curse, while my senses relive the light of the morning streaming through the open windows, the dozens of stimulating scents playing through the air, the feeling of desperate longing tingling through my skin, followed by the sound of the voice that plays even today and endlessly all around me, and the bitter taste that has grown into a vomitous coating upon my tongue.*

Yes, I remember it well; for that was the day my world began its slow crumble. That was the day the defective domino was unearthed.

***

"Good morning," I say, forcing a cheerful smile.

It's that time, again: time to hire a few interns. Bright kids, they are. All of them ambitious and smart, ready to take on the world and make a difference. At least they used to be. I'm not too sure anymore. I've been doing this for a long time, you know; and, truth be told, I have found myself losing interest in these bright new faces. As long as they do the job they're hired to do, I'm satisfied.

The name is Walter: Walter Edward People. I'm the founder and CEO here at People's Corp. I got my start overseas, working for a company called Georg3. But I have never been very big on not being the boss; so, I left the company and started People's Corp. Since then, I have grown into a globally recognized organization, with a market cap greater than that of Georg3, which I believe is now called Liz2y.

Now that we have gotten introductions and a tremendously abbreviated and woefully simplified version of my history out of the way, let us return to me sitting in my office with a bright-eyed, sharp-dressed, clean-shaven, slick-haired, peppermint-breathed, tailored-suited, summa cum laude graduate from Student Loan University, who is asking me, Mr. People, for a job as one of his trusted management interns.

They're interns, they really are; they're not technically in charge, but…oh, who am I kidding? They run almost everything nowadays. It used to be that I told them what to do. Now they mostly tell me what they're going to do. Most often their decisions are, I think, harmless enough that, should I disagree, any protest from me would, I feel, be a poor use of my frequent self-granted sabbaticals—raised eyebrows, an *ahem* or two, and maybe a few *tut-tuts* are about all I can seem to manage in most cases. I rarely make it to the suggestion box they leave out; though, one wonders upon looking at its rusty hinges if they've ever seen the inside of that box.

This is not to say they *never* hear or heed my words. There are times when I do complain, and complain loudly enough to make them throw up their hands and comply…well, in their own way and at their own pace they'll comply. Still, most of the time they just do; and do they do, with or without me.

Oh, well.

We're doing all right here at People's Corp.

The interns I'm presently hiring will fill the vacant seats in the central management office, and each will be hired to a termed contract. Keeping fresh faces in management is essential, but I have long suspected these kids are a bit like that one carnival game—I'm sure you know the one: where someone places a peanut under one of three cups and then shuffles them all up so you have to guess where the peanut is hiding; only, here in the People's Corp. management office, we have a lot more cups and a heck-ton of nuts.

There aren't a whole bunch of seats to fill this year, but still enough to have made me smash that snooze button this morning until it broke. This used to be quite a process. All the interns—either fresh faces or those seeking contract renewals—would battle each other with ideas, profound (or imbecilic) thoughts, and proposed innovations, until only the best were left standing—or sitting, I suppose…in a cubicle.

Weeding out the good from the bad was challenging work back in the day. It required a great deal of time to be invested into every intern. I had to study each one very carefully to ensure only the best and the brightest made it through to a seat. It makes sense, right? I'm hiring managers, folks to whom I'll be entrusting the reins of People's Corp. Investing time into each one is only logical. But it's a lot of work. And lately I've been relying just on my gut.

"Have a seat, Mr. Cheatem," I say, motioning with my hand for the boy to take a load off in the chair opposite my desk. "Let's see, here," I mutter as I put on my spectacles and look over the intern's application. "Mr. I. Cheatem."

"Ivan, sir," the young lad interjects.

"Yes," I reply, prolonging the syllable and gazing over dropped spectacles like a librarian. "Ivan."

I look back at his résumé.

"Top of your class," I say, reading his credentials, "president of student council, bachelor's degree in communications, master's in public speaking, regular volunteer at the campus soup kitchen, sixth-string pitcher for the baseball team, proficient horseback rider, recipient of the campus' coveted Masterious Equivocatus award for outstanding professional parlance; math club, chess club, glee club, future leaders club, a cappella contest runner up; and, last but not least," I say, executing a quick double take before looking placidly back at him, "excellent hand shaker and…baby kisser."

Placing the list down, I regard him diagnostically, and say, "Quite a list here, Ian."

"Ivan, sir; and thank you!" he replies, cheerful as a lark, looking very proud to have had his accolades and accomplishments read aloud to him.

"So," I continue, "what makes you People's Corp. manag—excuse me—intern material?"

"Well," he says, straightening up and centering his tie, even though it's already perfectly centered, "I'd like to point out, first and foremost, that you and I are really no different. Sure, my diploma may be a bit fancier than yours, my attire more expensive, my ordinance divine, and my friends and family more influential than the Pope himself; but I, like you, am dedicated to this organization, to seeing it continue to expand, to nurturing its development by—and let me stress this—any means necessary."

I'm not sure I processed all of that. In the strangest of ways,

I feel grossly insulted, and yet rather uplifted. Maybe I'd missed something. What a nice tie, though. How nice of him to wear a tie featuring People's Corp.'s colors! Still, for someone dressed so well, one would have thought he would have selected a color-appropriate tie *without* smudges on its face. Those two little black dots look like burn marks, or ink stains. And is that another streak of...

Perhaps I should focus a bit more on his answers—but, so far, I think I have a good feeling about this one.

I think...

"Very good," I say, nodding with the same thoughtful stare I'd maintained throughout his speech, though now it wears more as a mask to conceal my slight dubiety. "So, tell me," I continue, "if you were given the chance at a manag—*ahem*—intern position, how might you go about advancing People's Corp.? Are there any specific policies you might wish to amend?"

"I'm a big fan of policies," he replies in a rather pageant-esque manner; I've heard less enthusiastic tones win the tiara and bouquet, "especially *your* policies. In my humble opinion, People's Corp.'s policies are by far the best in the world. Honestly," he chuckles, "I can't get enough of them! And I can assure you I know what they are."

"Yes, yes, very good," I say, still nodding; "but are there any specific ones you feel might need tweaking? How about our energy conservation policy? You know, I have received criticism over the number of hours I leave the lights on in here."

"Energy conservation is an important issue," he replies hastily, "and should be discussed. Lights are a big part of who we are as an organization. Lights help us see things; and when we see things, things get clearer. And when things get clearer, we can see. *See?*"

Was that…was that profound? Or did a handful of my brain cells just short-circuit?

"All right," I say, blinking bemusedly, trying to decide how I feel about the answer, while also endeavoring to conceal this very real feeling that I assume one would receive from the grill of a speeding semi upon stepping casually before it. "What about supplies imports? Do you think I should revert to in-house manufacturing?"

"Another great question," he replies, pointing at me and nodding his head, as if I am a fourth grade student asking fifth grade questions. "We all need supplies," says he with a grin, spreading wide his arms; "am I right or am I right? Supplies keep us working efficiently; they give us the tools to do our job. I mean, I can remember once when I was in need of supplies. What did I do? Why, I went out and got some supplies! That's what I did!"

He pauses, as if listening to roaring applause in his head.

"Don't you see?" he continues, tapping his finger atop my desk and looking at me encouragingly. "It's not about the *whens* or the *whys*—it's about the supplies! And your question is one into which I'll most certainly be looking if I get the job as one of your intern managers."

What did I…what was my question? I can't remember.

"Great," I say reflexively, as my brain feels like it just got off a merry-go-round spun by a green, gamma-rayed giant.

Either he's the best thing that has ever walked into my office, or he's out of his mind about a mile and a half. I can't tell. He sure looks the part; he's answered all of my questions…I think—he hasn't hesitated, at least. He's eloquent, educated, animated; but is that the leader formula? I can't remember. It's been so long since I've been *really* involved in this process.

Here's an idea: let's see how he does on the really tough, controversial issues facing the company. This should tell me all I need to know.

"Well, Ian—"

"Ivan, sir," he corrects. "Ivan Cheatem."

"Right, right, of course," I say. "Ian—I'm sorry—Ivan, I'd like to know how you stand on some of the tougher issues."

"Absolutely," he replies, looking slightly reserved, the way I assume a flight attendant with a terrible fear of flying would look whilst reassuring passengers minutes before takeoff.

Perhaps he's not too thrilled to be going down this road.

They never are.

I lay on him the first sticky issue.

"Uh-huh," mutters Ian—I'm sorry—Ivan as he listens to each point.

There was a twitch in his eye—a small one, but a twitch, nonetheless.

The second issue falls from my lips.

Ivan repositions himself in his chair and mutters comprehensively as I speak.

The final issue meets his ears.

Ivan purses his lips and, staring into the ground, begins to nod. He nods so long and with such a bug-eyed expression (the kind one would see from a dead bug) that I wonder if my words had failed to become acquainted with his eardrums.

"What are your positions on these issues?" I ask.

"Well," he starts, tugging at his collar and wiping his brow with a timid smile, "I've made my position known on these issues many, many times in the past."

"I'm sure you have," I say, as a pause begins to grow between us. "Would you please just repeat for me and for the sake of this interview what you've previously said?"

"Absolutely," he declares, his voice squeaking a bit. "I believe in a fair and orderly system." Cheatem pauses briefly to clear his throat. "What we need is complete adherence to the rules put in place; but we also need to seek out ways in and by which to amend our rules, and make them more accommodating and fair."

Perhaps I'm not being as direct as I should be.

"So, on the first issue," I ask, "where do you stand?"

After a tremendously loquacious speech, Ivan finally offers his position on the first, then follows suit with the others.

We continue for a little while longer before our allotted time—known these days as my attention span—expires.

I thank him for stopping by, and let him know that he and I will be in touch—which is just a polite gesture of speech; I expect he and his fellow interns will be in touch with me, polluting my mailbox with their headshots and slogans, and my answering machine with their salutations and sales pitches.

With a bright and warm smile, Ivan extends forth a firm hand, and offers me a button and a bumper sticker, on which his name and face have both been imprinted. Every intern candidate insists on doing this. I can't even begin to tell you how many buttons, caps, t-shirts, bumper stickers, yard signs, and other pieces of pointless paraphernalia I have stashed away in drawers, so deeply buried and forgotten not even a particle of dust can reach even one of them and retain a memory of the name it bears.

There are still quite a few candidates to review. It's going to be a laborious process, I know; but the work they do, or are supposed to be doing, is essential to this company's overall success. I just hope this year's lot has some real winners.

I guess we'll see.

Chapter II
The First Day

I*t's a strange sensation, a queer reality, to have open eyes that see all, and yet nothing whatsoever. I am a man of reason, armed with common sense—as are we all...are we not? Thus, I knew something was wrong; something is always wrong. I had seen the writing on the wall, and I had been given its translation. When the roof creaked and dust fell from the rafters, I waited. When my effects were removed for safekeeping and necessary purging, I trusted. When my colorful walls were suddenly swapped for bars and ice replaced my soft, warm carpet, I took comfort in memory. And when I was helpless and infirmed, I accepted aid from the one who had helped me read the writing, who had assured me that the roof was sound, who had promised to act as a faithful steward of my possessions, and who had spoken through my bars the warming pictures of bygone days.*

The eyes of the snake-eyed domino had veiled my own. I was made blind to the masquerade and led to the edge of a cliff. A prescription glaze was forged and placed across my eyes that I might reach forth into the haze, seeing naught but clear skies and bright light, and there in the heart of the fragile structure that was my own creation place the debased domino and perceive it make all things new, while before the veil all that had been was lost.

***

So, I've decided to hire Cheatem.

What else can I do? I mean, have you seen the list of candidates? Who has time to invest *that* much attention into a decision? I need some intern butts to fill some vacant seats, and that's exactly what I'm getting. Sure, they may have earned their situations on the merit of their diction, dress, and dumb answers, which really do a number on one's attention: the dumber the answer, the more memorable the orator—which, when it comes time to decide, really makes the candidate's name rather conspicuous upon the page. But I think the potential for good outweighs the potential for bad.

I have rules, you see, and all I ask is that they're obeyed. Please don't quiz me on those rules, though. I'm not sure I'd pass the test; I wrote them a long time ago. My mission statement and brand essentials document detail respectively the whys and hows of People's Corp. They're displayed behind glass in the main foyer of the building for all to read. I expect my interns to thoroughly know those documents. I expect it, not in an enforcing way, but rather as a necessity, a hopeful given, because, as I've said, those documents are beginning to get a bit fuzzy in the old memory bank—haven't paid interest on that investment, if you know what I mean.

My interns are (so I assume, based on the nature of their interest and application) professionals, experts in my business, individuals who know the core of People's Corp. in so proficient a manner it eliminates my need to remember anything specific, or to worry my otherwise occupied head over the handling of central issues. I rely on their guidance to move my hand to the proper signing place when the time comes to sign.

I can't stress enough just how important these interns are to People's Corp.—with my mission statement and brand essentials document (and whatever acumen and savviness they possess that I have not the time or inclination to foster) as their guides, the interns help to ensure, preserve, and further the promises and advancement of my great company. And this is precisely the reason why I always develop a fit of self-loathing whenever I brush off this process—but it's *so* tedious! If there were only an easier way to ensure these interns could be relied upon to follow the rules, preserve the structure, and keep the train moving forward so I wouldn't have to keep basing hiring on what are feeling increasingly like whims, I'd be able to enjoy the spoils of my past toils without these periodical headaches.

There're several reasons why hiring interns is the most challenging job assigned to me. One example is the nearly impossible task of discerning and exhuming an intern's true character. Allow me to explain. I go into interviews assuming that every intern is lying to me. Once I eliminate that variable from my cache of concerns, I am free to weigh their academic achievements and work history. But even that's a headache. I mean, how is one expected to get any sort of read on a candidate when there exist so many conflicting statements regarding character and conduct?

For instance, every candidate's résumé features the name of the cliquey, hive-minded society to which he or she, usually during college, has pledged his or her eternal allegiance. Presently, most gravitate toward one of two popular houses, the first being Delta Nu Kappa Upsilon (ΔΝΚΥ); they're known by most as Deltas. The other majority tend toward the prolixly named Epsilon Lambda Phi Nu Tau (ΕΛΠΝΤ), colloquially called Gamma Omega Pi (ΓΩΠ), for short, or Epsis for shorter. There is also a handful of other, popular houses, like Lambda Iota Beta (ΛΙΒ) and Gamma Rho Nu (ΓΡΝ); but candidates from those houses, or the countless, smaller ones, rarely see their applications unearthed from the stacks of Deltas and Epsis.

These houses have great influence over each applicant, as well as those with whom they interact. An Epsi could be the purest individual on the face of the planet, with not so much as a jaywalking citation on his or her record, and yet a Delta will insist to the world—invest his or her entire summer, most often—lambasting the latter, casting convincing aspersions on the Epsi's character, digging up stories no one would have ever thought relevant, and making them pertinent, like how this evil Epsi once filled his soda at the fountain, but then sipped the top and filled again; thus, sayeth the Delta, will he do at the company water cooler, robbing poor Mr. People of his much-needed refreshment!

To pledge to a house also entails the reading of and complying with the house manual, which details the house's philosophy and principles, as well as the accepted vernacular to be used when addressing outsiders. They even implement a strictly enforced, color-specific dress code. In a way, they're like their own corporations, each with its own set of rules and regulations, and even a set standard designed to maintain consistency among members. This isn't inherently bad; but, in my experience, these pledged interns have a tendency to place their respective house's rules over my own; and no matter what I tell them I expect of them, they usually stick to their guns (except for the Deltas; they're not big on guns).

While valuable experience may be found by pledging, it does not make my job any easier. Dealing with the friends and distant acquaintances of applicants telling me how wonderful said applicant is, while rival houses chant that they're the devil incarnate, does not help me thin the herd; it's all pledge house-based. Recommendations and dire warnings sent to me from pledge houses often have little to do with the candidates themselves.

So, there I am: lost and confused, and really, really tired. It all just numbs the brain, you know?

Every vacant chair has at last filled. I may not have spoken with every selected applicant, but I'll take what lies on the paper, however little it is (and what actual *lies* they may be), and hand those selections a contract.

What else can I possibly do?

Let me rephrase that.

What else do I possibly *want to* do?

***

"Well, Ian?" I say as I waltz over to Cheatem's desk. "Are you all set for day one?"

"Ivan, sir."

"You've been what?"

"No, sir," he says, smiling patiently…at least, that's how I observe it. His smile is always the same; so, I must guess its significance based on the situation. "My name is Ivan, not *Ian*."

"Right, right," I say. "Ivan, of course. Anyway, have you gotten yourself settled? Ready for the next six years?"

"You bet, sir!"

"There's a great deal of work that needs doing. People's Corp. is still a thriving institution; however, if we are to maintain any sort of forward mobility, we must not depart our eyes from the goal or our feet from the path. We cannot waste any time."

"Understood, sir."

"I expect you to be attentive to the organization's needs. I've grown a bit weary of chasing down every little problem my-self—that's why you're here."

"Yes, sir."

"Check in with me regularly, if you like. I may or may not be available due to my rather hectic schedule. What with all the social obligations with which I must remain current and fo-cused—not to mention all the vacation time I'm still trying to enjoy—I'd say my days take my mind out of the office both regularly and effectively."

"Makes sense, sir. You've put in a great deal of effort to bring the company this far—I'd issue myself a few more va-cation hours, if I were you. Why, with such a fascinating so-cial sphere emerging all around us, one cannot be blamed for wanting to do a little exploring. And you must never lose sight of you—*you* are the most important thing, the reason why this company exists! Take all the time you require to invest into the pursuit of your own happiness. Leave the dirty work to us: the ones who actually know what we're doing."

"Yes, yes, thank you. It really is nice to—wait, *what?* What did you say?"

"I said we have this place under control, sir."

"Did you just call me incompetent?"

I'm sure I'd heard this. Didn't I? Didn't he just say he was somehow more competent than I am?

"I wholeheartedly believe," he says, straightening his already straight tie and growing his neck another two inches, while his chin begins to lift, as if searching for the source of some de-lightful scent drifting through the air, "that my experience and my unparalleled dedication to this company not only prepare me to face the challenges ahead, but also see to it that any and every challenge is seen through to a successful and all-around beneficial end—nay, progressive step!—for this great and beautiful company. This is why I'm here: to be who it is you need me to be, and more…much, much more. I will—"

"Yes, fine, Allen—Ian—IVAN! I'm sorry—Ivan. Yes, that will do. Thank you."

Whatever he'd said…oh, I don't *really* care. Even if he had called me incompetent, I can't exactly say he's too far off the money. I'm no real businessperson. How I ever got this company started, I'll never know. It was a fight just to get here, and it has been a fight ever since. If it were up to me alone, I wonder if I could keep this thing afloat. That may have been the idea at the beginning, keeping the lion's share of the power in my corner; but my confidence in my abilities has dwindled with time. The more of these Cheatems I've hired over the years, the more I have come to realize, mostly from their leadership and upward council, that I was never really fit to handle all the ins and outs of running a corporation. And though I'm not very fond of an intern telling me he's better suited for control over my company than I am, do I really have an argument?

"Well, Ian—"

"*Ivan*, sir." Again with the gracious-sounding tone.

"Right. Anyway, I'm, uh…I'm leaving this corporation in… in your hands. You interns, I trust, will act for me? You will abide by that which is detailed in the brand essentials document—for that, Cheatem, can I count on you?"

"Indeed, sir!"

"Good…yes. Okay, well, I'm off to skim through some photo albums and chatter with the birds for a while. Are you all set?"

"All set, sir."

"Great. It's been a long time since I've observed you interns—I've practically forgotten how this whole program works!"

I let out a chuckle, but my contracting abdomen feels less like it's filled with gleeful butterflies and more like it's plummeting to my feet.

"You needn't worry about this place anymore, sir," he says like a babysitter coaxing a newborn from its mother's arms, while his hands reach up to his neck and again straighten that perfectly centered tie…which, now that I look at it again, appears very much like the one he had worn to his interview; the color is a bit more faded than I remember, but those odd smudges…

"We've got it under control," he says, jerking my eyes back onto his. "Just be sure to stop back in six years to renew our contracts and pick up a button with my likeness on it!"

"Will do!"

I say those words enthusiastically, but just to be polite; I don't like the way they taste on my tongue.

My feet carry me across the room to the door, undecided the whole way whether they'd like to go swiftly or sluggishly. The ground feels as if it's either made of air, or situated somewhere ten feet down. I feel like I've just been fired, actually. And the strangest part…I think I'm all right with it.

Chapter III
The Performance Review

Imbeciles, fools, entrusted with responsibility; the incompetence they bring leads to the downfall of all. They are unproductive—counter-productive, even; they are wasteful of time and patience; they turn stacks of dollars into piles of IOUs; they create and nurture great ruptures amongst themselves and in a building's foundation; they are greedy and selfish, single-minded and corrupted; they are liars and thieves, two-faced criminals; they are the dominoes poised to topple the whole works. And from among them arises one particular domino, a most deceptively defective piece, that weasels its way in amongst the rest before falling right into the heart of the grand experiment, promising stability, security, and light, while it silently engineers and sets in motion a terrific razing.

What fortification is there against so determined a destructive force? How can anything stand upon such crooked, twisted, unstable pillars with so unyielding a desire to tumble? What else can a company do but crumble when its trusted team of so-called professionals become kindred enemies and hone their skills in the dark arts of sucking the institution's lifeblood, in the advancing of the erosion of the foundation's rupture, and in the deepening of the divide they have created?

How can one prevent those wobbly dominoes from destroying his grand and fragile, domino structure when the piece to hurl all others to their faces is by their own bodies encircled and protected?

***

"Thank you for coming, Brian."

"Ivan, sir."

114

"Of course—Ivan. I apologize."

"That's quite all right, sir."

The candidate's voice is a bit less commiserating than usual. "No harm done."

There seems to be, though I can't say for sure, as my auditory nerves are currently on autopilot, a touch of imperiousness in his tone—or, is that resentment?

"Though I dare say my name will not escape you for long."

I'm rather distracted at present, thumbing through all these tedious papers on this Cheatem fellow. Today is Cheatem's performance review. It's the day I get to tell him all that I have and have not appreciated during his tenure, and then either present to him an extension on his intern contract, or terminate and replace him.

Cheatem is the first intern on the list for a review. I did this on purpose. He's expressed great interest in moving up the ladder; and lately he's made such a fuss in the office that I have been unable to ignore his presence.

Some say the squeaky wheel gets the oil.

Lately, I'd say the quacking duck gets shot.

I haven't done an intensive review like the one I have planned in quite some time, where I actually sit down face-to-face with the candidates. I've taken up the habit of simply looking them over for signs that they still fit the brand; if they do (for the most part, at least), I renew their contracts.

Cheatem's case is different, though. I've been forced to take special interest in his performance.

I lift my eyes over my spectacles.

"Is that so?" I say, not sure what exactly he'd said, but recognizing by his inflection that this response (and the one in the offing) is most likely the warranted one. "And why is that?"

"I have a feeling I'm going to be around for quite a while, sir. My voice *will* be heard in this place."

My head had fallen back into the paperwork as he spoke, but I seem to have caught the hint that his expectations regarding the trajectory of this meeting do not match my own.

"I'm sorry." I remove my spectacles and drop them onto my desk. "I'm afraid I missed what you'd said. You're going to be *where?*"

"Here, sir."

"Where is *here?*"

"Right here. This place."

"The place in which, as you just said, if I heard you correctly, your voice would be heard?"

"Yes, sir. Right here. And my voice," he offers with a gleaming smile and what appears to be a supercilious tilt of the head, "though from these lips is it heard, is your voice, as well. It is the voice of this company, and it *will* be heard in this place, so long as *you* love the spoils of this business and the bounty *you* have yet to attain. I speak for you and you alone, using that with which I have been endowed, as a member of the only class capable to conduct and control companies such as this one. Your voice is mine, sir—and *I* will be heard."

That sounded pretty good, I guess. But the melody that just floated to my ears, though tender to the touch, was not, I think, as warm as was the tune's intent. It might have been steaming hot; however, I'm rather hung up—frozen, I suppose, to maintain this metaphorically affected flow of consciousness—on two words, words upon which I've been hung since they were first spoken: *right* and *here.*

"What do you mean when you say, 'right here?'"

My query creeps forth from behind my teeth, and my body inwardly braces for the impact of his reply, just as my fragile exterior would if I were watching a freight train speeding along the tracks, to which I am helplessly bound and gagged.

Cheatem offers a half smile, a smirk, that looks longer than those we call whole. The one side of his mouth is stagnant, while the other is slowly being pulled like a rubber band in a most unnatural fashion toward and into—yes, into—his ear. He lets out a tiny chuckle, and then surveys my office, looking intently at my plaques and trophies, as would an antique appraiser...or, interior *re*decorator.

His gaze falls upon me.

"Here, sir," he says at long last. "Right here...at People's Corp."

That's the right answer, but I don't like it—not the way he'd said it.

"Well, Cheatem, let's, uh...let's get on with it, shall we?"

"Of course, sir! But, first, I wonder if you might help me."

"Help *you*? How?"

"The interns and I have put together a proposal of sorts. We call it the People's Corp. Contemporary Obligatorily Non-negotiable Transfiguration for the Realizing of Opulence and Longevity Proposal. Basically this brief, two thousand-page document details how we, the interns, might further the goals of People's Corp. via a reallocation of certain resources and restructuring of ancient hierarchies, all while removing the burden from the shoulders of ownership via a rewarding relocation, and putting said—"

"All right!" I shout. "That's quite enough. Has this proposal gone though the proper channels for review?"

I couldn't list a single "proper channel" if asked, nor would I recognize one if I saw it. I just felt like this was the right thing to say in this instance.

"Absolutely! This piece has been in the works for quite some time. We're all very excited about it."

I thumb through the massive stack of paper. If I had liked reading, I would have been a librarian. One thing I do note, however, is the design beneath the authors' names: a white, rounded rectangle standing vertically, bearing a set of black dots, one hovering over the other and both separated by a horizontal, black line—like a snake-eyed domino.

Interesting.

I've seen that design around here somewhere.

This is not the first time a proposal like this has landed on my desk from the hand of an intern. They write these things all the time—it's the only product of their work that I see, really. But these things are so long and so tedious that I've gotten in the habit of simply looking at the abstract printed on the first page, or letting them recite to me the highlights. Then I thumb through the stack—my present occupation—and wait for any trigger words to leap out and smack me upside the head. If none do, and the abstract sounds useful or benign enough, I sign away.

But this proposal is giving me a bit of a bad feeling. I don't like the eager way Cheatem is looking at me, like my signature is a home run ball he's dying to crush out of the park.

Then again, he has always perplexed me.

Maybe I'm just a bit on edge, overreacting. Can I be blamed, though? Right now, all that's in my head is the proposal submitted into policy last year that ended up doing away with the lock on my office door and the relocation of my office supplies to a company-controlled supplies closet. Sure, I had been convinced that removing the lock on my door was a good idea, but I still insist the supplies part was not in the abstract, just like the part about a intern-monitored camera being installed in my office without my knowledge was never detailed in a proposal I'd signed three years ago.

Yes, I have gotten burned in the past from signing without thorough consideration…but there's something about this particular, portly proposal that's just not…

"All right, Cheatem," I say, looking up. "When can I get this back to you?"

"Now." He sounds a trifle offended by my query. "Now would be best, sir, so that we can get the ball rolling, you see."

I'd hoped I could buy some time to forget about this thing.

"I see. Well, Cheatem, I'd really like to——"

"I'm afraid there isn't time, *sir*. We need to push this through right away. The forward progress and security of the office depends on it."

"Yes, but if I could just——"

"You *cannot*, in good conscience, just *sit* here in the luxury of this office while the walls crumble about you! Just look at how vulnerable and helpless you've let yourself become over the years! Sign and we can put that silver spoon right back where it belongs and ensure you are once again comfortable and safe in your office."

So, am I in luxury, or are the walls crumbling around me? Those things don't seem to go hand-in-hand. But I agree with his assessment of my vulnerability. The interns who were supposed to act as my new lock are rarely here when I need them; but they regularly show up *after* I'd needed them. Still, this office is not exactly a dustbowl; it hasn't been ideal as of late, but it hasn't been cataclysmic, either.

"Cheatem, I just—"

"Think about what *you* need!"

This outburst sounds like the brood of intolerant impatience infused with ire and masked by altruism. Or maybe it *is* a sincere, solicitous spirit, justly indignant at my hesitation. I've never known him to be anything less than passionate.

"We've made your job simple!" he continues. "Just think about how much you won't have to think about this place! Once this document is christened with your blo—excuse me—signature, we, the interns and I—not you, of course; you needn't lift a finger—can commence this necessary transfiguration. It's all for *you*, and to *your* credit! *We* will handle the dirty work."

I hesitate for a moment.

I eye him carefully.

I gnaw my bottom lip as I draw a deep breath into my lungs.

I look down at the paper before me.

I take up my pen, fighting the tremor in my hand.

I sign the proposal.

Silence fills the space between us as the last drop of ink is scratched onto the page. Though my lungs still trap that last breath, I feel like I'm slowly, silently deflating. Looking at Cheatem, I wouldn't be surprised to find a hose running from me and into him.

"Thank you, sir."

"Now," I say. "Let's get on with review, shall we?"

Cheatem straightens his stiff spine and centers his negligibly off-centered tie—this one is looking more black than colored, as if it's the nearly forgotten memory version of that first tie… but those smudges…

Releasing the breath I'd been holding, I replace my spectacles onto my nose and commence another round of thumbing through his file.

I pause on a particular document.

This is the one for which I'd been searching.

"Uh, Evan?"

"Ivan."

"Yes, Ivan. Um, Ivan, I'm looking at your office record, your work log."

"Yes?"

"Would you say this is an accurate record of your service thus far?"

I hand him a collection of papers. He regards them intently and quickly.

"Yes, sir," he replies, returning the stack. "I'd be happy to recite an abbreviated version for you—a highlight reel, if you will."

"No, no, that won't be necessary. But, Cheatem, if this record is, as you say, accurate, it's a bit concerning, is it not?"

"How do you mean, sir?"

I present another document.

"*This* is your job description, Kevin."

"Ivan."

"Right. Anyway, this is your job description. Notice anything?"

"Sir, " he speaks, looking me dead in the eye, not taking or even regarding the document, "I can see that you feel there's some sort of an issue."

"Well," I begin, admittedly feeling a trifle less empowered, as he seems to have stolen the ball from my court, and is preparing to start draining threes, "you have a list of duties I expect you to carry out, you know. This description was put together long ago to ensure—"

"Let me stop you right there, sir."

My lungs are instantly robbed of air, as if his words were a vacuum hose thrust down my throat.

"I'm not sure," says he, "that *you* truly understand this job."

Wait…am I Walter E. People, or am I not? Of course I know the job, don't I? It's *my* job, isn't it? Was it not I who had created it for the furthering of People's Corp.?

"You see, you may think the job of an intern is as easy as just picking up a pen and composing action plans and strategies. But it really isn't."

It isn't?

"I have to deal with those—pardon my coarse tongue—*morons* from that *inferior* house, whose name I shan't utter for the sake of this carpet remaining vomit-free."

An unsettling, ireful spasm shakes his bones as he says the word "inferior."

"I can't get anything done! They're *always* in the way—literally blocking my path to the fax machine whenever I want to submit an action plan or strategy for implementation. They just disapprove for the sake of disapproving! And don't even get me started on *their* action plans! Why, they'd bankrupt this company so fast if my house members and I ever let a single word of that hogwash and hokum they call productivity proposals enter the fax machine!"

With that grievance, one would think no progress had been made at all these past six years. Now that I think of it, *has* any progress been made?

"But, all that aside," he continues, with what I hope was a calming breath, "I have made People's Corp. a much better place. That house of fools may bite and bite hard, but at the end of the day, my house and I bite harder!"

Nope. Not a calming breath.

"Just look around!" he shouts, shooting his arms upward. "The walls are still standing, are they not? That putrid, pathetic, pool of pea-brained parasites would have razed these walls in a second had it not been for *my* house! They seem not to understand this place as I do. And no one knows *you* better than I do, sir! Why, I'll bet not one intern from that house has *ever* paid a visit to your office!"

No one has.

The last time I saw Cheatem he was telling me what a great decision I'd made in hiring him—that was six years ago. He's popped up every now and then, usually over the company intercom, yapping with a voice that sounds like he's speaking through a megaphone about some sort of issue in the office with some intern or another. Usually they're little things, like an intern not washing his or her hands properly, not washing their dishes in the break room, or taking too many days off from work. I don't really know for sure. They all jump on the intercom every now and then to viciously attack their peers and emphatically defend themselves; but I don't pay much attention to their yelling.

But, no, to get back to Cheatem's point, no one has stopped by my office. No matter how many times they claim to know what Mr. People would want them to do in a given situation, no one has ever come to me for an opinion. Not that I'd be available, anyway. I have a lot to do, you know.

"Of course no one from that harebrained horde of hopeless halfwits have hever—excuse me—*ever* paid you a visit!" he shouts. "Why would they?"

Cheatem throws up his hands and then slaps them down on his thighs, heaving a most impressive, how-did-he-not-just-expel-at-least-one-lung sigh, before his body tightens, as if every muscle is contracting in unison, and begins tapping his temple, so violently I fear he's going to poke right through to the grey matter.

"They *think* they know what this place needs—they really do," he whines like exhaust being forced through a single, tiny hole atop the face of a waking caldera. "But no one from outside *my* house is fit to steer this ship. No one! Heck, they'd happily drive us into extinction, given the chance!"

Gosh, that other house sounds terrifying!

"So, with all due respect, sir," he says, giving me the impression that the pressure within the caldera has dissipated… or, perhaps, has reached the dreaded calm, "you can keep your job description—it doesn't apply in the real world of business. One needs to rely on intuition, not rules, to make it in this ever-changing marketplace. I mean no disrespect, but you just don't understand the business like I do—like we, the interns and I, do. Times have changed! It's a tough world out there, sir. We have no time to check a list of requirements made by an outsider! We know what's best and how to get it done. And we will continue to get the getting-done done so long as we're left to the getting by those whose concern is and should be only the product of the done."

124

At that, Cheatem rises from his chair.

"Thank you for your time, sir," he says, stretching forth a firm hand and pulling back wide his lips to expose his pearly teeth. "Much appreciated."

He then hands me a button, on which his face has been printed.

"We'll discuss a new contract this fall, sir. I've decided to enter the running for the soon-to-be-vacant seat of president of this company."

His smile widens even further—how, I don't know—and he saunters confidently, like a gladiator champion, out of the room.

I sit back in my chair, though I feel as if I've been thrown back, as though a giant hand had just picked me up like a child's doll and hurled me into the chair...that's how I feel.

Reflecting on this most irregular review, I begin to wonder if Cheatem is right. Maybe I'm not the best fit to run this place. No one else is Walter E. People—I own this place. But running it? I guess that's why I need interns in the first place. They're the professionals. Me: I'm just the outlet into which they plug to derive their power. I'm not as flexible or as capable as they in matters of business. I may be the outlet, but what good am I without a cord, right?

Then again, I worry about this Cheatem fellow. He seems to be getting a bit too big for his britches (if anyone still wears britches enough to have outgrown them). I've never felt so powerless in all my life. But maybe that's the sign of a great asset, a perfect candidate, someone I can trust to run the business in my stead, to represent me. On the other hand, he has not done one thing he had sworn he would do, much less anything I have asked of him. No good employee has ever had that on their record, have they?

Maybe it's not all that bad. Sure, I have complaints, but that's to be expected, right? I suppose the good outweighs the bad. How bad can it really be? Everything seems to be moving smoothly.

Doesn't it?

Chapter IV
The Promotion

his kind of thing is not supposed to happen...not to me. It's almost too painful to describe. Seeing it all fall down...this happens to other companies, organizations with deeply rooted flaws, backwards values, and misguided directions—not to mine. I knew at the very beginning that challenges would inevitably arise, challenges for which there was yet no name or face, but also for which a plan would be necessary. But I guess there are just some events for which one simply cannot plan. Against those who are determined to see their own ends realized over the advancing of the company that has been entrusted to them, forsaking that great responsibility I'd handed over to them, what hope outside of absolute failure does a company have?

I guess this is what I get for entrusting a defective domino to stand and uphold my design, to further it, to make it better, to...

...to do the job that was once my own.

***

I hardly recognize the place.

This season, which comes every four years, always turns the office into a madhouse. No one really gets any work done, and it's a bit frustrating. I suppose I'm less frustrated with the lack of output, and more peeved with the barrage of People's Corp.-colored banners on which giant, intern faces are printed and strewn about the building. One could figuratively drown in all this intern and pledge house promotional propaganda, and one would love to literally do so.

At People's Corp., I like to rotate presiding management. I think I'd started doing this as a means of keeping the company's leadership in line with the present direction of the company, and to ensure that none of my managers got any funny ideas about owning the place. But a lot of funny ideas have become, shall we say, company policies in recent times.

The title printed upon the soon-to-be-vacant chair is President. I'm still the owner, but this individual, with my assistance (should I be around to provide it), and the assistance of the interns, heads the company for the duration of his or her four-year contract. They're allowed one contract renewal, after which they can assume special company roles, like motivational speaker, or "qualified" instruction manual writer. Usually the seat of President acts as a siphon through which the life light is drawn; so, we like to ease the weary retired into low-impact roles following their tenure.

This year, no surprise, Cheatem is vying for the position. His face is literally everywhere. Seriously. He actually just left my office, having wrapped up the recitation of his qualifications and the presenting of a syllabus of his proposed presidential actions, all before attaching to my suit jacket a lapel pin bearing his likeness, hammering a *Beat 'em with Cheatem!* sign into my redwood floor, and leaving behind an audiocassette player with a tape playing on repeat his megaphonic voice, saying, "*Ivan idea! Make Cheatem president!*"

I have absolutely no idea what that means.

After tossing the lapel pin, uprooting the sign, and smashing the cassette player into dust (I think he specifically chose an audiocassette because he thinks it meets me where I am: old and out of touch—a point I perfervidly resent), I creep into the hall like a soldier stepping onto the field of battle without a weapon. All around I hear shouts of praise for candidates from every pledge house, screaming the name of their chosen one, while berating and chastising pledged opponents. With so much pride and animosity among respective groups, one would never guess they all work for the same company. They've got team spirit, that's for sure; but they have no People's Corp. team spirit—none, that is, in which their rivals are or can be a part.

Though I'm not much of a fan of this circus and would much rather be occupying myself trimming the hedges at my social club, or chasing and catching imaginary cartoon creatures scattered about my office, it's up to me to pick a President; and, thus, I have to pay some attention. Thankfully—and I say "thankfully" with equal and paradoxical parts sincerity and sarcasm—these candidates make it nearly impossible for me to be ignorant of their parade. Their respective existences, their taped back smiles, ivory teeth, and inflated chests are like the eyes on those portraits that follow you about the room, that latch onto you and don't let go. No matter what I do, their cacophony will find me.

How does one escape such madness?

***

There's a great deal of blood on the floor. I've grown desensitized to this. It happens every four years, and I'm getting used and indifferent to it…perhaps bored is the word.

When at my door, every candidate is annoyingly charitable and nauseatingly cheerful. But they know I'm not fooled; that's not their point.

If you want to see what these candidates can really do, look no further than the dark and forgotten corners of curiously abandoned rooms—bloodied bodies of battered candidates from smaller houses, whose soapboxes could not lift them above the mob of their pledged opponents. These weaker candidates fall by the wayside, having never really had their voices heard; their legacies run red over the hands of their mightier peers, who move now to maul yet another of their brothers standing against them or their chosen one.

Having made my way through the valley of streamers, decorated ficus, multi-colored confetti, and burning effigies of rival candidates, roasting the raw carnage on the floor nearby, I happen upon a cubicle wherein Cheatem and another intern are battling it out.

It's a brutal sight.

Candidates used to debate ideas, policies, and things of that nature, offering an education on their views for the company's advancement and needed reforms—at least that's always been the idea. It was originally meant to be a presentation and exchange of intellect, reason, and logic, designed to inform and inspire, to change minds with honesty, with principles, with a demonstration that what is being said is intended to further the cause of the company—not the individual's quest for power—and discover truth.

But now it's a gladiator match.

No joke, at this very moment Cheatem is rolling around on the floor, hurling slavered insults and wild fists into the face of his rival, who is returning the favor with equal vim. Blood is everywhere, and in it stands a mob of supporters from both sides, cheering like apes and scooping up handfuls of blood to drink.

Maybe it's always been this way.

I can't remember.

This whole mess eventually proves too much for me, and I re-tire to my office to brood over the ridiculousness of this pro-cess and wish for a swift conclusion. At this point, I don't care who gets the President's chair. It's not like it will make much of a difference, right? Let them kill each other—I'll be reclining at my desk, snapping my fingers and chatting from a duck-faced mien into the wind.

***

"Sir?"

Honestly, the concept of peace must be a myth!

"What is it, Dyson?"

"Ivan, sir."

"Yes, Ivan. What do you want?"

"What *I* want is irrelevant, sir. I'm here because of what *you* want."

"I don't want anything, Simon."

"Ivan. And of course you want something!"

"But I didn't call you. Why so eager all of a sudden to know what I want? You didn't return any of my calls during your six years here at People's Corp.—all I ever got was your imperson-al away message! So, why now? Why are you so eager now to know what I want that you're barging into my office while I'm relaxing?"

"I have truly served you well, sir—you know that. Of course

you know that! Surely there is no doubt that I have served you well."

"Define '*well*.'"

"No need, sir," he declares with a tone that affects my skin the way oxidation affects steel, while straightening that same, smudged tie, now darker and more noticeably shifted from center. "My record speaks for itself."

"I should say it speaks volumes; however—"

"However, that's not why I'm here."

This is maddening.

"I'm here," he continues, "because you need me."

"Maybe I did, but—"

"More than ever, sir, you need me now. This company is on its way into the ground; but if we band together, you and I, one organization under my authority, we can bring this place into the stratosphere!"

Just then, before I can process that snide comment about my company being two seconds from a destructive impact and a fiery death, not to mention his audacity to suggest he deserves supreme authority, a loud ringing noise is produced into the air between us.

I look, and there on my desk, blanketed in a dense forest of cobwebs and beset with rust is an old-fashioned, rotary telephone. The corroded receiver dances atop its base as it rings, kicking dust into the air, while the discolored dial wheel rotates freely, slowly, past every number. The sound is terribly loud, piercing. I'd never before noticed it there. Has it always been there? It's hard to tell, but I think this phone might have been... I'm not sure, actually, what color it might have been; so much has faded. Almost everything has faded, as a matter of fact, except for the manufacturer's label, which reads *Able Champion's Telephones, by Independent Operators National.* I'm not sure if I've ever made a call, much less touched this annoying thing.

I reach for the receiver.

"Thank you for your support!"

Cheatem bursts in front of me, takes my outstretched hand, and begins shaking it wildly. For some reason, I don't know why, his enthusiasm reminds me of a deep-rural pig farmer, who's pig has just won *Best in Show*: the coveted blue ribbon.

He's the farmer, but I'm not the judge, you see.

No, I feel like the prized pig.

"I can't tell you how much your support means to me and to this company!"

I am completely confused, and yet I can't seem to remove my hand from his. Not that he's gripping too tightly—I'm just not feeling as if I can. And, oddly enough, that's all right with me. He must use lotion, or something. It's like my fingers have found a nice, warm womb in which to rest.

"I'm going to do everything in my power to make this the greatest company there is! What do you say, friend? Are you ready to help me?"

Again, the phone rings. I can't extract my hand. The ringing sounds fainter this time. It's not as loud as it had been.

"There!" Cheatem declares. "Perfect fit!"

Walking back around to my front after an unnoticed departure and absence, Cheatem places both hands on the arms of my chair, gets close into my face, and opens his mouth wide with a smile.

"That's better, isn't it?"

There's something in my ears. They feel—I don't know—full,

I guess, obstructed. It's kind of nice. It's kind of *nice*. It's *kind* of—

"Nice, right? No more distractions! I'll be sure to speak louder and keep my lips close so you can hear me, though that with which you've been fitted is designed to pick up only my voice— no outside noise!" says Cheatem with a chuckle. "But don't you worry; all you'll ever need to hear will come from *these* lips. I'll keep you informed about the goings-on and company updates. For that which I know you need to hear, and for filtering out that which will cause only unsettling, uncomfortable stirrings, you can count on me! You know," he continues, looking like a stagy infomercial actor posing his thoughts to his inept acting partner, "I think this chair might be a bit stiff, don't you think?"

He takes me by the chin and starts nodding my head up and down. Actually, I'm in control—he's just guiding my dumbfounded, captivated face.

"Exactly! Why not try this one?"

Instantly, I'm in a new chair: a luxurious, ultra-padded, black leather chair. Its padding must be made from some sort of magical material, like the wool of shamanistic sheep, or cotton fairies, for as I sink deeper into its abyss of tranquility, I feel as though any stress, any worry, any negative emotion, is fading away—not leaving me, just fading, as if a tarp is covering them: a tarp of blissful ignorance.

The phone rings again. Its call is softer, but it's enough to shake my focus from Cheatem's face. I lock my eyes onto the jingling device, and raise my hand to—

"See!" Cheatem declares—screams, actually. "The chair vibrates! Isn't that comfy!"

It really is. I like it. I like it so much in fact that I move to adjust the vibration speed to something a bit more suitable to my comfort ambitions.

"Ah-ah!" Cheatem cries, wagging his finger back and forth in front of my face, looking like a mother tenderly scolding her toddler. "This building has only so much power—we must make sure not to use more than our share! I think this level suits you just fine, don't you agree?"

Even though I think I disagree—though I'm sure he knows more about these chairs than I do; it was he who had made the recommendation, after all, and implemented it under my posterior—I cannot lift my hands, or even my legs.

Snapping out of what feels like a train of thought chugging through a sea of molasses, I realize that my wrists are bound to the chair by leather straps, and that Cheatem is fastening tight the last notch on my similarly restrained ankles.

"Perfect!" he cheers. "Don't worry about a thing, sir. As long as I'm around, you can rest easy! I am your humble set of arms and legs! You needn't bother yourself with the grueling task of lifting even this little finger of yours," says he, taking my pinky and wiggling it, as if he's telling me how it went to market, "to keep this company going. Writing new rules is intensive work for the hands. Keeping tabs on the inner workings drains the legs. That's why I'm here! I'm your new appendage system! It's time to have your cake and eat it too! Just leave the baking and the serving to me!"

Not a bad deal. Who wouldn't like perpetual comfort? And cake—now I want cake. Where can I get some cake?

The phone rings again. I can't hear it, but I see it rumbling.

My eyes widen and panic shoots through my body as I realize how difficult it will be for my restrained frame to reach the phone before it again stops ringing.

"Well!" shouts Cheatem, as he grabs hold of my face and presses his nose into mine. "How silly of me! How can I expect you to relax with all these distractions playing wildly about you?"

A toothy smile grows on his face...and it keeps growing. For a moment, as I watch the skin of his cheeks split in two, sending misty explosions of crimson over my face, my heart is filled with terror. But then, suddenly, Cheatem's fingers gently caress my eyes, softly closing my lids.

"Just ease into your own, little world," he whispers into my obstructed ear, which still hinders that which is not his soft and reassuring voice. "I know you have a dream, don't you? An ambition. The People's Corp. dream is in us all, and I am inviting you to sink right into it. Stay there while I build for you that which is in your mind. Let Cheatem construct a world just for you, in which you might thrive while happily lost in a dreamland paradise. Just be sure you never open your eyes, lest the dream fades away. I'll take care of everything."

With that I feel his fingernails dig into my ocular cavities, piercing through the lids and imbedding into my precious eyes, before they are quickly ripped from my head and, I can but assume, discarded—or worse, consumed.

I don't feel any pain. And, honestly, I don't really miss my eyes. Is that not strange? The world into which I've drifted, wherein the dream after which I've sought my entire career is true, the one far away from my office, though populated with the safety and comfort my office provides—that world is far more enjoyable, far more peaceful than whatever reality in which I had long been living. In the strangest of ways, in an almost unconscious way, I am content, and maybe...maybe even a bit grateful.

The phone rings. I can't hear it, I can't see it, nor can I reach it; but I can feel it. The vibrations are so violent that I can perceive them crawling though the vibrating chair. They are distinctly different from the chair's vibrations. These are coarse, jagged; they feel as a day's hard labor feels on the hands, like they will make a callus of my entire body should they persist.

Though I am reluctant, the compelling nature of the phone's rumbling is moving me to speak. I call out to the phone, hoping the receiver, though unengaged and impossibly distant, will hear my voice and send it where it needs to go.

"Whoa, there!" I feel a hand slap across my face, over my mouth. "Let's not over-exert ourselves! You needn't worry about lifting your voice! I'll speak for you! That's why I'm here! Just give me your voice."

I feel my jaw slowly, but anomalously with and without my conscious will, opening, guided by what feels like Cheatem's finger.

My tongue is pinched.

It feels like two fingers are pulling gently on it, stretching it to full length.

"That's right," he says palliatively, like a dentist who has at last located the pesky cavity and is about to strike. "Just a bit further."

Suddenly the vibration level on my chair is cranked to full blast. The sensation is so overwhelming, so climatic, that I almost immediately surrender to its power, disregarding, forsaking whatever fear had momentarily taken me, whatever consequence I had in the offing foreseen.

After hesitating, and all at once, I give myself willingly and eagerly over to the pleasure of the chair, and explode with unmatched euphoria, which causes me to clench my entire body and violently clamp my jaws together…completely severing my tongue.

As blood fills my mouth and trickles through my chattering teeth, the vibrating chair ceases to vibrate.

"Thank you for your support."

Cheatem is behind me, now, speaking softly, slowly, calmly. His hands are on my shoulders, massaging them with a comforting rhythm, but with fingers like knives.

"It's a brand new day, sir," he chuckles. "Time to get to work."

With that, I feel his hands release my shoulders, and then, with an agonizing but silent snap, the back of the chair breaks in half, sending splinters and a hard, horizontal, wooden slab into my back.

I've never been so uncomfortable.

"Don't you worry about a thing, sir."

Cheatem's voice is getting softer, distant.

"Everything will be fine."

***

"It's time, sir."

I must have dozed off suddenly.

"What?" I mutter, blinking my eyes in an attempt to recover the room.

No answer; just a piece of paper on my desk.

The guy who delivers this particular paper every four years comes and goes so quickly that I hardly have time to register him. I always seem to be looking out the window or making coffee, or doodling on a notepad whenever he enters saying,

"It's time, sir."

Anyway, the moment is here, just as he'd said. It's time for me to submit my selection for People's Corp.'s new President. What I do is simple: I just make a pick and submit. There's a great deal to consider—many voices in my head to heed is, I think, the best way to describe it; and every one of them brings up a lot of urgent points. No one candidate ever fully steals my heart, but one will eventually find enough favor with me to assume the chair.

It's time, now.

I pick and submit.

Walter E. has spoken.

***

I'm reclining in my office, casting spitballs against my wall, and reflecting on days past, the kind I long to reclaim after the President's chair has been filled, when the office operates at its usual level of insanity: a level easily ignored.

"How nice it will be," I say, chuckling to myself as I think about the folly of the campaigning season. Those interns sure can tear one another apart. How they ever work together after these ordeals I'll never know.

Maybe they don't, actually.

Maybe they don't.

Cheatem enters my mind, and I let out a single, airy laugh through my nose and shake my head. He's one of a kind, that Cheatem. Can't say I've never seen anyone like him, because I have; but he sure is up there on my top ten list of—

"*Attention!*"

It's the intercom. My selection has been processed. It's time for the announcement.

"Attention, People's Corp.! Attention! Your new President has been selected!"

I lean forward and stretch. It will be nice once my pick gets into office. I think they'll bring about some much needed change. I really think they'll do some good, hopefully.

The announcement continues, and the name is declared through every room and every hallway of People's Corp.

And I can hardly believe my ears.

Chapter V
The Initiative

When did it happen? You've got me there. I have been on this path for so long—it's hard to pinpoint exactly where and when things began to fall apart. But I certainly know how and why it happened.

It certainly is a strange sensation, a queer reality, to have open eyes that see all and yet refuse to see anything. I once believed myself to have been a man of reason, armed with common sense. So, why, when I knew something was wrong, did I hesitate, justify, and ignore? Does a man of sound mind seek a translator when the writing on the wall is so ominously clear? Is it reasonable, sensible, to hesitate when inside a crumbling building, assured against instinct and mounding mass of drywall debris in one's hair that the structure is sound? Is it commonsensical, rational, to justify a burglar's plundering on the basis that he claims to be a gifted home decorator, who is merely exercising his craft as a favor, discarding that for which he knows the rightful owner has no use and promising to keep safe in his own abode all the rest? Is it logical, levelheaded, to find oneself inexplicably and impotently in a cage, only to ignore the bars, the cold stone floor, and the smell of freedom just beyond one's reach? Would one label oneself a pragmatic, sober individual, who, upon finding oneself in chains, arms and legs nailed to the floor, accepts gladly the tonic offered from the hands bearing also the rusty dust of linked steel, the red of spilled blood, and the battered hammer that drove the nails?

A strange sensation, and I know it well. It is a self-inflicted feeling, a self-inflicted effort. And it begs the question: Why?

Why?

Because, it's easier.

It's easier to let it all fall down than to build it up; it's easier to shake one's head at the rupture in the foundation than to mend it; it's easier to point the finger at the incompetence of others and say that the fruit it bears will be out of one's hands and their fault; and it's easier to deepen the divide and hasten destruction by refusing to lift one's benighted, lazy eyes to see what one has created.

I was wrong about dominos. Now that I have had time to reflect, it seems one need not wait for a single piece, pristine or flawed, nor the careless hand that places it, to destroy the structure. Dominoes are doomed to fail. There is no design made with dominoes that can withstand their own nature. It makes me wonder, then, why anyone would labor so long on castles of this kind, why anyone would put his faith into something so feeble…especially if the hand that places is itself a domino. How foolish: a domino seeking to build a structure more perfect than itself using only itself.

But, I guess, it's all I have right now.

Or, maybe, it's all I choose to have…all I choose to know.

It's my fault. I should have been more than a collection of dominoes; I should have been a stack of solid bricks; then no domino, however corrupted, could have toppled me. But the bricks that I had been when I began were eroded by my apathy, my carelessness, my ignorance, and my tolerance for darkness, until all that remained were dominoes; and by the domino was I felled.

None but I must shoulder the blame, for none but I had been granted this great responsibility; in my laziness I had cast it all to the dogs, and by my own hand I was made blind to the writing on the wall—the literal writing on the face of that snake-eyed domino I had placed on end in the heart of this withered and weakened creation.

It was all right there. Black and white.

I need a revolution.

No. Revolutions are man's beloved curse, his sacred master, his corpse bride. A revolution means simply to go from Point A to Point A; and I have ever revolved. I am dizzy; I am faint—always turning, going nowhere; the dizzy make up the dead. My hands are empty; my body is numb. I had thought I was climbing, but I was actually spinning. And spinning out of control I have lost everything. I had sought new ground on which I might construct the greatest company there had ever been. But I have failed. I have not climbed. I have merely revolved, and in so doing I have reproduced the very thing from which I had departed.

I need something else...something I once knew...something I have willingly erased...something that will make this right, even if doing so means razing this hideous, dizzy mess.

The ground beneath my feet has given way.
Helplessly though the abyss I fall.

Heaven, help me.

Walter Edward People

***

"It's right here, sir. And this *is* your signature, is it not?"
"Well, yes, it is; but—"
"Then there's nothing to discuss."
"How can I be banished from my own building?"
"You're not being banished, sir. Of course not! You're being

relocated."

"Relocated? You said I was being evicted from my office!"

"Yes, correct. It sounds like we're on the same page, but I'm getting the sense you might actually be a chapter or two behind."

"This is *my* office! *Mine!* This is where the owner, the guy whose name is on the jumbo sign attached to the roof of this building, resides!"

"*Used* to reside, sir. You're being relocated."

"Where on earth else am I—"

"The basement, sir. You're being moved to the basement where you might be more productive, more useful to the new order of this company."

"Excuse me? Where?"

"The basement, sir. Your new position will be stationed in the basement."

"*New* position? No! This is ridiculous! I'm not going anywhere! This is *my* office, *my* company—I am the supreme authority around here!"

"About that, sir…you're not."

"What?"

"You're no longer the supreme authority."

"That's impossible! What on earth are you talking—"

"The People's Corp. Brand Agreement, sir, is very clear on this matter. See?"

"I know what it says! I don't have to read it!"

"I'd advise you look at it again, sir. See here, item seven dash one of the People's Corp. Brand Agreement, to which *you* voiced your affirmative support, signed, and submitted for implementation at the inception of People's Corp., says that, and I quote, '*Supreme authority to govern and make decisions regarding but not limited to the advancement, management, organization, and operation of People's Corp., shall hereby be entrusted unto the sole entity of founder and owner, Mr. Walter Edward People, as heretofore granted upon the formation of People's Corp.; and that authority shall not be impeded, obstructed, shared, or removed in any way, shape, or form, unless so granted under official, written consent.'"*

"Right! And I don't consent! I've *never* consented! This is an outrage!"

"Actually, sir, you did give written consent."

"What?"

"On page one thousand twenty seven of the People's Corp. Contemporary Obligatorily Nonnegotiable Transfiguration for the Realizing of Opulence and Longevity Proposal, it states that, and I quote, *'Should the supreme authority of People's Corp., as defined by item 7-1 of the People's Corp. Brand Agreement, assign power to another entity for, but not limited to, the purpose of steering People's Corp. toward the realization of any goal,'* which this proposal, by its very nature and definition, does, *'he shall consequently assign all power to that entity, thereby entrusting supreme authority of People's Corp. to said recipient, regaining authority only at such a time deemed suitable by the party unto whom it has, by said proposal, been forfeited.'*

"That's pretty straightforward, is it not?"

"I…I don't know what to say."

"No need to say anything, sir. President Cheatem has asked that you submit to him, in writing, your formal letter of congratulations and compliance before the end of the day. I trust you can handle that and the collecting of your personals unassisted?"

"Wait, what?"

"A letter of congratulations and compliance, sir. Simply stated, President Cheatem wishes you to compose for him a message of good will and well wishes for his promotion, along with a statement of compliance, saying, basically, that you accept your new role and willingly release the responsibility entrusted to your former title. President Cheatem has plans to reorganize People's Corp.'s internal structure and will be rewriting the Brand Agreement; and since your name will appear not in that agreement where it once had, nor will this new structure afford your previous chair the significance it once held, I have been asked to shake your hand firmly, thank you on behalf of People's Corp. for your years of service and continued support, and escort you to the escalator—taking first your letter, of course."

"My name appears nowhere? My name *is* the company!"

"That may soon change, sir. But, like I said, that's no longer your concern. Now, if you will please be quick about that letter."

"And what if I refuse to write such an abomination?"

"It's really just a formality, sir. Your signature on years of intern proposals is consent enough; I can just inform the president that you're pleased with the change of pace if you'd rather not say it yourself."

"This is unbelievable."

"Not really, but I understand the sentiment."

"How did this happen?"

"You'll have plenty of time to mull over that quandary once we get you settled in the basement. Now, c'mon, gather your effects. I'll take you to the escalator."

***

When did it happen? When did I start to lose control? How could I have let all of this get away from me?

I guess I'd thought People's Corp. was invincible, impervious to the failings that have plagued so many other companies. The management model I had created made so much sense and had worked so well for so long; I suppose I forgot just how to keep it running. I wish I could say I've been betrayed; and maybe I have been, but whom can I blame before me? Did I not grant those who have now taken over my beloved company and hurled me into obsolescence the power they now wield?

Indeed, I had.

Cut down by the sword I'd forged.

Poetic.

Pathetic.

Apathetic.

Interesting how those two words work: pathetic and apathetic. My apathy was indeed piteous.

I could not believe my ears the day Cheatem was declared President of People's Corp. I'd wondered for days whether my hand had actually written what I'd thought it had. To hear his name… unbelievable. But that was only the beginning. It took many years for me to learn the truth, that what I had perceived as control was nothing more than an illusion. It was like riding on a stationary bicycle: pedal as hard as you like, you're going nowhere. Funny, as my life consists now only of riding this rusty, squeaky stationary bike—*Pedal for Power and Your Portion*, they say. Pedal for your meals, else you starve and those dwelling upstairs have to find a new way to keep the lights running.

I had turned my back on my company for so long I was unable to recognize what had happened. And now look at me: reassigned to the cellars of People's Corp. Who would have thought the owner would occupy such a space as this? To be honest, I don't remember this building ever having such a space. A suspicion arises that it may have been built without my knowledge.

They brought me down here by way of a single escalator—a really, really long escalator. The trip was surreal. I couldn't believe what was happening. And now I can't find the escalator to go back up. Not like it would matter. I seem to remember hearing my escorts saying something about orders to set the escalator to a permanent, downward trend, and then bolting the doors at the summit. Had they done so, even if I could ascend a descending escalator, getting back into the main office would require some door-smashing, brute strength, and determination I'm not sure I possess.

It's dark down here, dreary and damp. Everything is basic, plain; just stainless steel tables and chairs, built solely for functionality; no imagination or comfort above the absolute bare minimum, which—taking into account the proverbial warm-feather-bed-slash-jumbo-sugar-laced-pacifier from which I've fallen—actually feels more like absolute zero...maybe even a little less.

There's barely any light down here. Nothing works—not the microwave, not the refrigerator. Even the faucet sprays rusty water at a rate and with a consistency of a drunken hurl.

What's worse, though, is my new uniform. While I don't particularly enjoy wearing clothes that feature Cheatem's emetic, smiling face, set in the middle of my shirt, and polka dotted along each pant leg, the "Cheatem Trifecta," as I call it, is far worse.

First, there are the Cheatem glasses. They're like sunglasses, only the lenses are filtered by Cheatem's face, which obstructs and distorts my world, sometimes making it impossible to walk. Everything is blurred, basically. Next, there's Cheatem Radio, which is played through headphones imbedded into my ears, and locked with what feels like tiny padlocks that loop through the mechanism and a piercing made through the back of each ear, holding in place the earphones and the arms of the sunglasses. This arrangement holds everything firmly onto my head in a nice, molesting manner. The radio station is stellar, too. All day I get to hear Cheatem's vomitous voice, spouting daily nonsense I endeavor to ignore.

And finally...well, this is the worst of all. I would have gladly taken all the rest and more if only to be spared this one. On the day of my reassignment, Cheatem's henchmen forcibly restrained me, and then proceeded to sew my mouth shut with a stitching made from a strange fabric. Comparatively, I'd hardly noticed any of the other elements, like the radio or the glasses, being attached; but of this one I was acutely aware.

That pain was worse than anything I've ever known.

So, what do I do here all day? I've already mentioned my new job—they call me a Manual Power Generation Specialist. What an insulting title. I ride this stationary bicycle until my legs turn to wet spaghetti and my lungs start pulling at my ribs for something with which to cut themselves free from my windpipe. In doing so, I generate power for the offices above me and earn performance-based points that, when I've earned enough, call forth a morsel of food to be delivered to me.

The food I earn is basic. If my scores are good, it arrives once a week in sealed bags, either dried or frozen. The worst part is when the toaster oven fails and I have to eat this cardboard unprepared; and to eat it is to mash it up until it becomes a powder or a paste that I can force through small gaps in my sewn lips.

My new job also consists of various, menial, manual labor tasks. Mostly I'm washing the dishes that get chuted down from above. Seeing a decent leftover scrap on a plate when I open the chute door is like a jolly, bearded elf in red bouncing out of a chimney. (Actually, that sounds terrifying, but I think the point is made).

I've been at this for years, now. Every day I reflect on the past— the most I've thought of the past in my history. Only now do I realize what it truly means to be powerless. When I'd had the ability to make change, I chose idleness. And now I'd give anything to at least leave a suggestion in the suggestion box. I can't reach the suggestion box from here, and whatever comments I try to send to the main floor are never answered.

How did I end up here? The musty air and this greyscale world, wherein the only company are the echoes of my muffled laments, have been eating me alive. I think I'm going crazy! Most days, when I'm not biking or washing dishes or emptying the trash, I'm sitting on my metal chair at the metal table, surrounded by rows of other metal chairs and tables, staring at a red blur that has grabbed my eye every day since my arrival, a red blur with a golden streak painted upon it. It always looks so far away. And every time I see it I tell myself I'll investigate tomorrow, for today ever finds me weary from the eternal hours.

I'm always thinking. What else is there to do? I think often of a time gone by and wonder—wonder so incessantly that I'm sure anyone listening to my thoughts must be fed up with hearing it—how on earth I have ended up down here. There are many nails in the coffin I'd built for myself, but the one that mobilized my journey to this place was that darned People's Corp. Contemporary Obligatorily Nonnegotiable Transfiguration for the Realizing of Opulence and Longevity Proposal.

How clever is that Cheatem.

I didn't see it at first.

I'd never read between the lines.

The People's Corp. *Contemporary Obligatorily Nonnegotiable Transfiguration for the Realizing of Opulence and Longevity* Proposal.

Those are a lot of fancy words.

It was right there all along.

How could I have missed it?

Clever, Cheatem. Very clever, indeed.

And right on the money.

But even that—though the physical, legal catalyst to which I can point in thanks for my new situation—is not the root of the problem. Can I blame the interns? I'd sure like to, naturally. I mean, a great many of them did actively weave their treachery into all those proposals I'd signed over the years, providing the vehicle by which I could effectively and unwittingly forfeit my power to them. But—*confound it!*—I should have paid attention! I should have investigated! Not because the interns were inherently unworthy of trust, but rather because it was *my* duty to ensure the safety of *my* company, the security of *my* authority! All I ever did was sit back and accept the gentle pacification of those I'd employed to do what I'd become too lazy to do myself! Sure, I'd needed them—I'd needed them to echo the words and actions of their boss. But when that voice is silent and those limbs have atrophied from lack of use, what else can I expect?

Oh, but what was I if not a wild horse in need of reining? Without trusted guidance, I might have run this company off a cliff! For that, the institution of internal management was legitimate…right?

Perhaps that's a flawed notion. Perhaps that wild horse knew where it had wanted to go—it had just needed the reins to keep it on its chosen path. Maybe I am just a wild horse, and that's all I'll ever be—and maybe that's what People's Corp. had needed. Or maybe I'm just not a horse at all. Maybe I'm just plain old Walter Edward People: a flawed collection of passion and purpose, who doesn't really know (or want to know) what he wants or what he needs, but who knows now what he knew long ago: that I am human, and as such I can labor toward the light, or with ease destroy.

That's why I had founded People's Corp.: to give myself the chance I could never have had under any other roof: the chance to choose the path on which to set my feet, unbound by force to the path of another; to choose the easy roads toward transient thrills and perishable prosperity, or to challenge the steep and strenuous routes, pursuing truth and preserving the choice to continue the difficult climb, or to slide comfortably toward the road that leads to a master.

Now, here, at the very end, when all has crumbled, when I have reached the depths of my comfortable, suicidal slide, Walter E. People is at last ready to work.

But where do I begin?

What exactly do I do?

How can I…?

Wait a minute…

My old mission statement!

I have it right here!

Cheatem's posse had tossed it down the garbage chute some time ago for me to rescue from the refuse. And, here—here is my brand essentials document! Oh, when ever would I have thought that one day I would be lifting thanks to that snake, Cheatem!

Gosh, when was the last time I'd looked at these documents? These words—was I ever so eloquent, so conscious, so focused on this company's goals and promises? I needn't ask how; it's all right here! How to bring proper functionality to People's Corp.—it's all detailed right here in this beautiful, brand essentials document! And reading this old mission statement, my letter of resignation to the owner of Georg3, penned long before I had welcomed the Cheatems of the business world to infect this corporation with their subtle poisons—reading this reminds me just why I had set out to build this company in the first place.

Yes, this is what I need!

But how will I regain what I have already forfeited?

I am ready to work, but…

I have to go back. I have to take that first step.

C'mon, legs! I know it's been a while since we did any uphill walking; but we have a long way to go, and I can't do this without you! Ready, dear hands, for the task ahead will require your undying labor! Lift, my eyes! Set your gaze upon the hill, where sits your home, beset with vandals and thieves! And rise, my voice! Let those who would see you banished hear your cry! Let them learn of my return long before I appear on the horizon! Let them fortify their dark towers with their feeble darkness and lies, for I am armed with right, and will see their shadows laid to ruin upon the dusty earth!

Walter E. is rising once again.

It's time to complete this revolution, return to Point A whence I came, and there set a course for Point B.

My hands reach up and slowly coil about the earphone padlocks. Sucking in a gust of air through my nostrils, I, with a closed-mouth, clenched-teeth yell, yank the padlocks from their holes in my ear, severely ripping the flesh.

Casting the bloody ensemble of earphones, glasses, and ear fragments to the floor, I, with nails long from years of unimpeded growth, slice through the stitching woven into my lips. It's arduous, agonizing, but also necessary. Many times I lower my hand, acid tears falling over my face. But with every gulp of air my lungs draw in through new openings, openings that have for years been sealed, I become all the more emboldened, craving another gulp.

I weep and I wail, but I do not waver.

Finally, my lips are free.

A pile of shredded, blood-soaked, black and white fabric rests at my feet. I take a deep breath, as streams of crimson rain from my lips and creep along my tongue. The air tastes stale, but at least my mouth is now free.

The awful sounds of the basement, forbidden for so long, now assail my ears, sounds that are enough to drive a person mad—high-pitched sounds, like nails on a chalkboard, or forks scraping along a plate. Everything around me slowly comes into focus. I knew, but never *really* knew until now, just how vividly forsaken my recent home is—and now I can clearly see what lay under that red and gold blur in the distance: a door with a golden handle.

It's the door to the escalator.

It's my way out of this place.

I take another deep breath.

I am ready.

I'm going back.

***

My hand is on the door. There, through a window in its center, I can see the escalator that had years before taken me to this place. It's still running downward, rapidly, at breakneck speed. At the summit sits my ravaged, oppressively remodeled home. I must reclaim it. What lies ahead is no easy task, but a task, nonetheless, that I must face.

I whip open the door. That was the easy part. Now I have to ascend this descending escalator. These steps are just flying! How am I ever going to mount a massive flight of stairs, one that covers over two hundred stories, that's fighting against me? It's hard enough climbing a descending escalator moving at normal speed—but this is just crazy!

But it's the only way.

I have to try.

Tenderly, slowly, I lift a foot and carefully place it down upon a step. Immediately that foot is whisked away, sent packing before it even began, and I fall forward with crushing intensity onto the metal steps, which then fling me onto my backside and right back to where I'd started.

I do this several more times, amassing an impressive collection of scrapes, gashes, bumps, and bruises.

Stepping rather dejectedly away from the seemingly insurmountable mountain, I limp back toward the door to my prison. As I reach for the handle, my eyes catch my reflection in the window. The escalator steps have crafted me as would the hands of a contemporary art sculptor, whose use of black and blue hues, and streaks of crimson to fill the rips and tears in my clothing, the sides of my face, and the space between my lips, would doubtlessly elicit enchanted *oohs* and *aahs* from gallery hoppers, along with intense queries about the message behind the piece that is me, playing out in pompous tones that ponder, "What do you think the artist is trying to say?"

Perhaps that artist is saying I'm not fit to reclaim what I have lost. Or, perhaps, and possibly inadvertently, that artist is telling me that recapturing the right and freedom to be who I was is no easy price to pay.

This will be far more difficult than it had been when I had broken away to build this place all those years ago.

But I will be a pile of pummeled pulp before I quit.

Whatever I'm doing, it's not working. Time to try something new. Nothing is going to stop this escalator so long as those above are at the controls. The only thing left to do, I suppose, is to take a leap.

One.

Two.

Three!

Having propped open the door and paced backward all the way to the other side of the basement, I race as one eyeing the gold medal at the end of the run (or, perhaps, the last flat-screen TV on Black Friday), and then leap with all my might onto the escalator.

My jump has put me further up the stairs than any of my previous attempts combined; but I've not succeeded just yet. Wasting no time, I begin scurrying up the rapidly descending steps, running on all fours like a lion, bounding like a kangaroo, and sweating like a vegan in a meat cooler. I'm exerting every ounce of energy I have in store, keeping my eyes fixed upon the summit; determined, though my fingernails are ripping from my battered hands, and my feet keep slipping on steel and blood, to make it to the top.

My days in the basement are over!

I will *make* it so!

Just one more leap, and I'll be…

Made it!

I've done it!

I have beaten the escalator and reached the doors leading into the main floor!

Chains and locks are woven through the door's golden handles, but they will not stop me. Though I am exhausted, I have strength enough to continue, for this is *my* company, and no one—*no one!*—nor any barrier set in place to imprison me shall over me prevail!

I lift my pummeled body from the ground, face the doors with a furrowed brow and hunched shoulders, and take a deep breath.

"Cheatem!" I scream, as I charge through the door, shattering the chains and locks with my indignant ire. Armed with my name, and all that had from that name laid the very foundation on which I tread, I storm inside and shout again, "Cheatem!"

I call *his* name, but it is for all those who have broken their contracts with me that I seek.

With a wild kick, I break down the door to the management office, wherein I find several of my former interns huddled around a throne of raw, rotting flesh, over which plates of shimmering gold have been draped in the shape of a chair; they are fused to and supported by golden rods driven through the carnage and into the floor. Some of the interns wear chains, others don robes of luxury, and all are offering their reverent servitude and allegiance to him who sits upon the throne that has by the blood of his peers been forged, and beneath a mighty crown, crafted from the bones of opposition, and dressed with the stains of my own silence. In the left hand of this towering figure is a torch made from the molested bindings and pages of knowledge; in the right is clutched a bloodied axe.

His name is Cheatem, and he is my creation.

"Cheatem!" I scream, as I stomp through the doorway.

"Well!" the elevated, former intern returns, speaking—as I perceive it—hollowly, feigning the manner one would typically assume when greeting a dear, old friend.

As I approach, a pair of henchmen block my way. Horror grips me as I survey the faces of my obstructors. They, all of them, are blind. Some have had diamond fragments forced into their eyes; others bear empty sockets. Their lips have been stitched shut with black and white fabric, just as mine had been. Their heads are bare, their ears fixed with Cheatem Radio transmitters, and their limbs—their poor, feeble, sickly limbs—are bound with barbed wire, around which the flesh has regrown. Their hands are forced to clutch tools of labor, while their feet are encased in blocks of cement fixed to large, turntable-like platforms that roam about the room, directed by a device worn on Cheatem's wrist.

They're hideous, and I fear them; but more than that, I pity them. And, worse still, I see in them...

"Why!" declares Cheatem with a wide, wicked smile, though any onlooker, not diagnosing as I am the active agent pulling that smile upward, would surely say his is a pleasant appearance. "If it isn't my old friend, Mr. People! I trust you have been enjoying your new position. Must feel rewarding to be so useful to the company for a change, eh?"

My blood is boiling.

"You—"

"Ah-ah!" he interrupts quickly. "Please, Mr. People," he says, lifting his hand to me after resting his axe on the one side of his throne. "This is a *safe* place, you see. There are no hurtful words permitted here. Nor would I have *you* raising your voice."

Pulling back his long, purple robe, he turns and examines his throne carefully, inspecting quite closely one spot in particular along the edge of a gold plate, before turning again to face me.

"No," he says, grasping at the knot of that now tar-black tie, drooping so far from center, and pulling it clumsily back into a near-center position; it's so dark that the smudges have completely disappeared into its void; "I would not have you raising your voice, here. Could be," he takes a deep breath through his nostrils, and I think I see him shudder slightly, "destructive."

Stepping down the staircase made quickly by the backs of bowed interns, he glides to my side, drapes his arm over my shoulders, and points ahead with his torch.

"Come!" he shouts proudly, eagerly. "I have something I would very much like you to see."

"I—"

In an instant I am on the floor, writhing in pain, while Cheatem, looming over me with a bloodied, ring-speckled fist, glares diabolically—eyes ablaze above clenched pearls, glistening between wide, wickedly smiling lips—and calmly says, "Please keep your voice down, sir. I *really* don't want to have to tell you again."

Just then powerful hands hoist my aching frame from the ground, and I am handed over to two henchmen, who each wrap their bound arms around one of mine, completely immobilizing them, and begin leading me through the halls, following Cheatem's voice.

"I want to show you the future," says the leader of our little parade, as we sail along a dimming hallway to a set of giant double doors. "For years, long before I was ever granted an intern position, I had been planning some specific changes for this company, changes I knew and know will bring about a new and exciting chapter in our history, one that will stand and be revered for countless decades to come! And now that I have finally, with your absent consent, made possible by your years of dedicated distance from this organization, razed every remaining barrier, dismantled every last institution and policy that had long defined and inhibited a place soon to be formally known as People's Corp., my vision—a forward-thinking, revolutionary vision—can finally be realized.

"Welcome," he shouts, as we burst through the double doors and into a large, circular room, one I do not remember commissioning or constructing, "to the *Cheatempire!* The new and improved Cheatem Works Unlimited, where prosperity is our highest priority—prosperity through unity; unity through equality; and equality through sacrifice."

Closing his eyes, he bows with a smile. The moment seems to suggest, by his protracted stay in the bowed position, that applause is desired. But he will receive none from me—although, I'm almost positive there's a tremendous chorus of praise ringing in his head.

"What I have done—plan to do, rather—," he continues, standing upright, "what People's Corp. was ever unable to do, is basically sever the chain that had long held the feet of *your* corporation, sir, in bondage: the chain of unnecessary, debilitating risk, ever fixed to the stake of free enterprise."

Cheatem, who had taken a brief, wide stepping, moseying stroll about the space, turns quickly to face me, placing his nose nearly on top of mine.

"You *never* let yourself understand," he snarls, whispering sharply, while his one eye twitches and a wicked sneer quavers on his lips, "how impotent you made this company by allowing its parts to squander what talent and resources it had, all in the name of personal gain. Your eyes were lost, *always* lost, in the abyss of leisure afforded by wealth. You cared not for this company, only for yourself."

His face slowly retreats.

"Well," his voice is low and resentful, but quickly gaining volume and impassioned momentum, "now he who will see equality for all, he who has the courage to enforce company-wide fairness and instill collective understanding, healing the poisoned minds that had so long by your misguidance believed in a dream of plenty, of a life filled with overabundance; now he who will bring about the change this company needs has finally taken control! Witness the realization of true production and just fulfillment!"

Had he not placed himself so close to my face, forcing me to regard him, every word he just said would have been lost on me, for I am completely captivated by this room. It is enormous! How such a beast can fit inside the walls I'd built long ago—this I cannot fathom.

It's like a gigantic balloon filling up within these walls, threatening either a devastating demolition or a deafening pop. I feel as though I am standing in the center of a gigantic metropolis, a megacity—in the very center, surrounded by the remains of a fallen civilization, on whose bones this new, dark, and terrible empire has been built. This place has both the size and spirit of such a scene.

Towering, golden torches, with white flames burning in black bowls set at their peaks, line the walls of this goliath room. The white flames give the room a strange, red hue, one that illumes in detail only that which stands in close proximity, at about an arm's length. All else is a distant, red haze.

I am led toward the center of the room, which I am beginning to understand is a three-dimensional map of sorts, a blueprint of Cheatem's ambition, his plan for remodeling my company. I see cubicles filled with stoic faces, all fixed with the Cheatem Trifecta, tinkering away at grey tasks. They are indistinguishable from one another and unimpressive, but equal. They're horrifying. And worst of all, they look exactly like me.

Numerous security cameras pollute every workspace, and no office is fitted with a lock. As a matter of fact, I don't see any doors, either. At every cubicle, fixed to the undecorated, plain, grey walls are red, fluorescent signs, all featuring arrows of direction and words reaffirming the value of one's assigned labor. A despondent pace is maintained among the horde. They seem unable to do anything but sit and produce. But worst of all, they, all of them, every last one of them, are connected to a grey, spongy, umbilical cord-like wire that runs from their mid-sections to the ceiling, where all wires converge and connect to a large half-circle with a central tip. The object appears to be forged of bright light. It's so hard to see. One cannot gaze upon it at all. I wish I could see what's inside, what color it is, what upon it has been written—anything.

We finally arrive in the center of the room, where we find another circle. This one has a diameter about as long as I am tall, and in the center is—

"That's my mark," says Cheatem, proudly. "It will be gracing every hall, every ceiling, every everything once I'm through re-modeling. I even had it crafted into my crown."

He did, indeed.

I hadn't noticed that.

I gaze upon his shiny hat for another moment, and then divert my eyes to study the mark on the ground. Now I know what the fabric was that had sealed my lips. It was a rag bear-ing this mark. The circle in the center of the room has another circle at its center—a black circle, in the middle of which sit two white, rounded squares, one stacked on top of the other. A black bar that runs nearly as long as they are wide separates both squares; and in the center of each, the very center, is a single, black dot, a burn mark, an ink stain…a dark smudge.

This design…many times have I seen it but have failed to see it.

I know exactly what it is.

How fitting.

A drop of blood from my mouth falls upon the design, just

below the top square's dot.

"I see you've been exercising your jaw," says Cheatem, as he stoops down to wipe the spot with his thumb before it dries. "You really shouldn't have removed that stitching—it's twice as painful the second time around."

"There is no pain," I growl, "like living with them sealed, Ivan."

"Well!" he cheers, jumping gaily to his feet. "Look who finally got it right!"

Taking me by the cheeks, he thumbs playfully, mockingly at my shredded lips, wiping the blood he's just retrieved upon the surface whence it came.

"But, no," he says, intimately studying the vacant holes littering my lips, before forcibly gagging me with a black rag bearing his mark, and covering my mouth with a thick strip of duct tape, which he wraps about my head. "You're wrong about that. And you would not think it so had you ever lifted your eyes from inside yourself.

"You see," he continues, draping an arm over my shoulder and tilting his head, nearly resting it on my cheek, "under *your* control, this place was rife with turmoil and unnecessary pain, caused mostly by untamed lips. But now, this place is free of such problems, thanks to Mandatory Communications Management, as I call it. Because I know this business better than it, or anyone else, knows itself, I am able to speak in the one voice this place was ever unable to form. Now, with no opportunity to argue or deride, or lift anything potentially hurtful or damaging about this place or anyone under this roof, or hear or see anything offensive, I have secured the safety, security, and happiness of all."

Words escape me. Not that I can speak, anyway.

"So, as long as I hold the reigns," he proceeds with a grin, "command the wheel, push the pedals, so to speak, this place will run smoothly.

"For instance, you remember all those supplies issues People's Corp. used to have? Remember how some drawers would be full of sticky notes, and some penholders would be full of pens, while others had virtually nothing? Pen pilferers ran rampant, and those supplies wars were devastating! You remember, right? Oh, stop it—yes you do! Well, those days are no more! Now, everyone will get the same amount from the same source: Ivan Industries. And for that supplies-supplying service, all will see the same amount automatically deducted from his or her paycheck—paychecks that will comply with my new wage equality policy, which will eliminate jealousy and resentment by paying a flat rate for all services. No one will own the supplies; I've abolished private ownership. But that fee will allow them to borrow what is required.

"With that, revised wages, and my new Warm Hug, Open Hand cultural model, where everyone will be assigned equal value, and those with inherent, superior value will gladly, by official mandate, share the spoils of that value with the whole staff, the Cheatempire will surely thrive!"

We continue through the room. Cheatem struts confidently and casually, while I quarrel with the grimy rag stuffed in my mouth.

"This," Cheatem declares, extending a proud hand presentationally toward a wall of storefronts, "is Ivan Industries Avenue! This is where I print paychecks, where paychecks are cashed, where health services are distributed, where groceries can be purchased—etcetera, etcetera. Cheatem Banking, Cheatem Health, and Cheatem Supermarket are all provided under the new benefits package at Cheatem Works Unlimited! And here's the best part: Because all paychecks are issued as Cheatem Credit, valid only on Ivan Industries Avenue, one needs not fret over perplexing, frustrating options or competitive pricing! Talk about convenience!"

I make a deep, grunting sound, and attempt to scowl my words to life.

"I can see you don't quite appreciate the value of Ivan's Avenue," he says, walking slowly to my side with his hands folded behind his back. "That's all right; it'll be hard for everyone, at first. Growing pains," he sighs, shaking his head, "are an unfortunate part of, well, growing. It won't be easy to get everyone on board, but I'm confident that with a little time and persuasion,"—these words trickle off his tongue like a serpent slipping over the cold face of its kill, while from his pocket he lifts a set of brass knuckles, which he tumbles about gently with his fingers in a conspicuous, reflective manner—"everyone will eventually come around. Like horses, you see," says he, looking up and replacing the knuckles in his pocket. "Gotta break 'em in if you're ever gonna lead 'em to water. And they'll drink, all right," he chuckles to himself, glaring fiendishly, with dark pleasure, at his torch. "They will drink their fill, indeed."

We circle about some more, but I have seen all I need to see, more than should be witnessed by anyone.

Sweat pours down my face as I observe the remains of my beloved company, as I look helplessly at what it has become, what will soon from its ashes emerge, deceitful and ugly. This is a dark, desolate place: grey and barren, devoid of the light it had once born, reduced to a painted skeleton, and ruled by the very mind and body from which this disgraced businessman had fled, so many years ago—a mind I once thought was far from my own, but which I now realize was at the core of my very being.

I'd wanted this. Not *this*—not this darkness. I'd wanted what I had thought the path I'd chosen—the path I now know leads ineludibly to this very place—would bring. I had said I'd wanted control, but my actions (inactions, rather) begged for a master. I had sacrificed control for security, peace of mind, leisure. I had wished for ease, but my apathy pleaded for suffering.

This is what I had wanted.

I just didn't know it.

I don't want it anymore.

"Thanks to you," Cheatem laughs, slapping me in the chest with the back of his hand, as we return to the center of the room, "I have been able to make all of this possible! And thanks to you and your continued support—and by support I mean faith enough to let me run the show—the Cheatempire will be the standard by which all companies the world over are judged.

"In this business," he grins, "all roads lead here. You were the exception for a while, sir. Boy, were you the exception! But yours was just a dream; there never was any real foundation. Your company was the slapstick comedy before the feature presentation, the clown act before the play, the jester in a hall of kings. Yours was an entertaining run, a bucket of laughs; but, in the end, when the material finally runs dry—" a most wicked chuckle oozes through Cheatem's glittering teeth, and with speed like summer lightning he snatches my neck, pulls me close to his face, and sharply whispers, "—off with his head."

I am led back to the throne room. Cheatem glides gracefully to his seat and takes up his axe, placing his torch into what I assume is a cup holder on the right arm of the throne. My heart thumps wildly as he approaches me, dragging the stained steel across the stone floor, making it screech eerily. All the while he's looking at me from beneath a knitted brow, with eyes like those of Claudius the night he moved to slay his brother.

He stops; the steel ceases to scream.

"I need you," he whispers, after taking me gently by the back of the head and placing his mouth nearly into my ear.

He exhales a small laugh.

"Say it. Say it, sir. I have done right by you. I have. Even under your ancient structure, I did right by you. And yet you never spoke those words with your lips."

I can feel his cheek brushing up against mine. His free hand pets the other side of my face in a most violating manner, turning my blood to ice.

"Daily," he purrs, "while at your desk, feet elevated, thumbs occupied, gaze captivated in worlds of fantasy; daily, while lost in dreamland, living a hallucination, chasing a delusion; daily, while scoffing in my direction, while expressing your discontent with our work, composing complaints upon sticky notes strewn about your polluted wall," he snarls, as grave intensity and barely bridled passion creep into his voice, mounting slowly in volume; "daily, while sitting, idly passing the hours, lifting not a finger of investment into the cogs of People's Corp.; daily, sir, I watched you; daily did you silently scream your need for me, for all of us; and daily did I wish that one day you and I would be *here*," he shouts the word as he jerks his body away and strikes me square in the stomach, "and that *you*," another shout as he kicks the back of my leg, sending me crashing to my knees, "would *beg*, on your *knees*, while I looked upon you as you ever did me, for my *service*; and that *you* would confess unto me, without reservation, those *beautiful, empowering* words!"

Pain pours through my nostrils as I try to recover my breath.

Cheatem leans forward, cocking his head to one side and regarding me maniacally—eyes wide and quavering; cheeks trembling, and mouth slavering.

He raises his shaking hand to my taped mouth, looking like an eager child on Christmas morning reaching for his presents. A finger nearly touches the tape when he suddenly stops, smiles pleasantly, though I know it bears nothing pleasant within, and lets out a sigh that seems to take away his maniacal jitters.

"No," he mutters. "You've done enough to make any confession from your lips irrelevant."

Standing upright, he looks at me with parting eyes.

"Goodbye, Mr. People, sir," he says professionally, dispassionately, coldly. "May you find fulfillment in the cellars of Cheatem Works Unlimited. And," he continues, picking up his axe and resting it on his shoulder, "may I never have to clean your blood from my blade."

With a flick of his hand, I am hoisted to my feet by the henchmen—who, I must admit, were incredibly resilient and diligent in keeping my upper appendages restrained all this time—and dragged toward the escalator. My body is aching and my heart has not stopped sprinting since I'd whipped open my cellar door.

As I watch Cheatem glide toward his throne, I am conscious of an approaching tidal wave of emotion. Throughout the tour, waves of fear and anger had crashed over me, producing shivers and palpitations of the heart…and, most of all, sweat.

I am soaked.

Terror and rage so powerfully and so continuously beleaguered my very being with every realization of a new and terrible alteration to my company, and the ever-present, haunting revelation of what I had done, that I feel as though I've just taken a forty-foot dive into a tub of water. And now that I'm being dragged away, now that my failure has to me been revealed in full, and any chance of reclaiming my home is slipping away, this tidal wave of fear, sadness, panic, fury, and a hundred others, is closing in rapidly.

The henchmen push through the doors.

The shadow of the tidal wave looms.

And as beads of sweat and frightened tears rain down my face like a waterfall, I notice something.

The tape…it's loosening.

My sweat and tears, and the blood on my lips are weakening the adhesive, eating away at its binds!

My eyes widen and my head, which had dropped to my chest in despair, snaps forward. Unable to use my hands, I begin rotating my jaw, pushing on the rag with my tongue, doing whatever I can to remove that binding strip before we reach the escalator.

Almost have it.

Almost there.

Just a little bit more.

Got it!

"STOP!"

My scream echoes like a sonic boom through the halls, and immediately the henchmen grind to a halt. The shock of my outburst has left them momentarily stunned, and I use this opportunity, as well as a borrowed supply of adrenaline, to wrestle my arms from their powerful grasps.

To my surprise, they put up little fight. Without thinking on it further, I spring to my feet and sprint for the doors, looking back only once to see the mobile platforms on which the blind henchmen stand sparking violently, as if short-circuiting.

Blasting wildly through the doors, I scream, as I had before, only now with a far more impassioned volume, "CHEATEM!"

All eyes lock onto me—all heads, rather, and empty eye sockets, for those so situated.

Cheatem, having gripped the arms of his throne in utter shock, begins tapping the device on his wrist, sending forth his henchmen.

"Restrain him!" he shouts.

Henchmen on sparking platforms rush toward me, but they cannot maintain a true trajectory, and I will not be restrained. Armed only with my fists, I fight off the feeble army, until none but Cheatem, the interns cowering at his feet, and I remain staring at one another.

"Have you forgotten the one for whom you work?" I scream, as I slowly approach, shoulders hunched and fists clenched.

Ripping the duct tape necklace from around my neck, I cast it at Cheatem's feet.

"Have you forgotten that you work for *Walter Edward*, the *People* of People's Corp.? HAVE YOU?"

My voice lifts with a volume I had never known it to possess. Let's hope it lasts.

"Sir, please!" Cheatem begs, scurrying his legs onto his throne and drawing them to his chest.

He frantically studies his chair, looking mortified and hugging it, as if trying to hold it together with his eyes.

"Stop yelling! Please!"

"I had asked you to lead, to help guide this company; but you have razed these walls that were built with *my* sweat, with *my* hands, by me and for me—all for your own gain! You have failed me, as I have failed myself! You have failed this company! But no more! That failure ends today!"

As my voice continues to amplify and my blood burns hotter with a consuming resurgence of the power I had foolishly given away, I see Cheatem looking about quickly, to the left and to the right, appearing more unnerved and panicked than I have ever seen him, while the deafening sound of crackling fills the room.

"Just, please, sir; stop screaming! An arrangement can be made! Certainly we can—"

"SILENCE!"

I yell so loudly I leave even myself in awe.

Cheatem lets out a tiny, toddler-like yelp.

"I will hear no more of your treachery! I am putting an end to your reign! I am taking back People's Corp.!"

The power surging within me is intoxicating; the temptation to give into chaos is overwhelming.

Cheatem pulls the ends of his cape around him like a blanket, and holds his crown close to his chest.

"No, sir!" he begs. "Please *don't*"

"Ivan!" I bawl, louder still. "All of you!" I say regarding the group. And with a sound like the blaring of trumpets from a celestial orchestra, and a gust of air so powerful I'm sure they'll name it Hurricane Walter, I roar, "YOU'RE *FIRED!*"

At once the throne on which Cheatem sits shatters into a million pieces and he, his crown, and his royal façade come crashing to the floor.

With thunderous steps, I approach the trembling collection of interns and their now impuissant leader.

Looming over them, I fire a vicious glare into their petrified eyes, and snarl as I condense my ire into a single growl.

"Get out."

***

My hand is on the door. There, through a window in its center, I can see the escalator that had years before taken me to this place. It's still running downward, rapidly, at breakneck speed. At the summit sits my ravaged, oppressively remodeled home. I must reclaim it. What lies ahead is no easy task, but a task, none-theless, that I must face.

My hand is on the door…

Outro

WHY is it not *Outroduction?* We have the informal *intro* and *outro,* as well as the formal *introduction*—so why not a formal *outroduction?*

Grammatically it would make sense, I think. The word *introduction* comes from the Latin *introducere,* which is a combination of the prefix *intro-,* meaning, "to the inside," and the suffix *–ducere,* meaning, "to lead;" thus creating the literal, "to the inside lead"—more simply put, "to lead to the inside."

Now, if an introduction literally leads one into something, then why can't an *outroduction* lead one, as the prefix suggests, out? I think we need a formal antonym for *introduction;* therefore, I am submitting the word *outroduction,* along with the word I'd invented in this book's introduction, *novelic,* meaning "of or relating to a novel," to Mr. Webster. And get ready, sir, for I have plenty more new words strewn about several of Conners' novels. Once those puppies are published, I expect soon after to see a new edition of your dictionary hit the shelves.

And, now, to business.

Yes, dear reader, we have reached the end.

One thing remains: an ending.

A good ending brings all the elements of a story together; it reveals the truth behind the secrets that had driven the plot to its climax, ties up loose ends, and teases potential future tales. A good ending can make or break a book—but how does one end what has been not a continuous account, but rather a potpourri of various narratives, each with its own unique path, purpose, and destination? Am I just supposed to thank you, dear reader, for reading, and then send you on your merry way—a simple goodbye after everything we've been through together?

No.

I can't let you off that easily.

Not that I have to worry about doing so. Just read the copyright page at the beginning of this book, the page over which you always skip, never paying any heed to what has there been written. Go ahead—take a minute to read that page. I'll be right here when you get back.

Now that you are aware of your "legal" obligation, allow me to give you a proper sendoff.

Because the writing of an ending is such a sacred task—one that, for any story, requires a thorough understanding of and devotion to the plot, setting, and characters—it has never been up to me to do anything more than copy and paste what the Author has composed to conclude his masterpiece. Sure, I may be asked to tweak a few lines, here and there, to make them a tad more flowery than the systematic, fact-driven tone submitted by the Author, often times translating bullet points into a whole narrative, and in so doing maybe actually write what most would call the majority or even the entirety of the book. But I never—let me stress this, *never*—write an ending without any guidance whatsoever, without some sort of understanding as to where the denouement must commence and conclude. There are many elements in the novels I narrate that are wholly my own; the conclusion is never one of them.

Which is precisely why I was so shocked—flabbergasted, completely dumbfounded—when Mr. Conners informed me—he didn't ask me—that I would not only be introducing and composing interludes for his seven works, but that I would also be writing the ending.

Perhaps you don't quite understand the weight of carrying another man's work on your shoulders to a point of completion, whereat you must safely deposit all that has been written, gently and rather adroitly, onto the head of a pin—the single aim of the production, from and by which all else stems and will be judged—and there make it balance.

How can I explain this?

Imagine the great Egyptian pyramids. Now imagine one of them is a giant, pyramid-shaped water balloon. Now imagine you have to drape that water balloon over your shoulder, climb to the top of the largest of the pyramids, and there, tip to tip with the pyramid, deposit the water balloon while making sure it doesn't burst, tumble away, or lose a solid, pyramid shape.

It's kind of like that.

But I have never been one to shy away from a challenge.

Here goes nothing.

G.O.T.I.T™ *Brain Reader Activated*

Good heavens, this is harder than I'd thought! How many hours has it been? Nine? Ugh, I'm getting absolutely nowhere! What am I going to say? What can I do to wrap this up? "What can I do to get to you and find a way back to your—" no! No time for boy band ballads! Gotta focus! All right, now, the obvious, cliché way to wrap this up would be to say that all these stories are about something, that they have a common theme—and that theme is…is…liiiiiiife.

Yeah, like no one has ever done that.

"Yes," say some, "this pretentious piece, proficiently produced, perfectly portrays the plight of the planet's personages, the passage of periods of pleasure and pain, and pompously proclaims my preeminence and power over pedestrian peoples who pay to praise my products!"

Push off, you pontifical—no; don't pay insult with insult. Though I am just talking to myself, so is this technically masochism?

Anywho, since simply stating that these seven stories (must stop alliterating!) center upon life would be in no small way a cop-out that would greatly diminish the quality of what has been compiled here—Oh! But I've just thought of another alliteration! The letter 'L!' I could say the stories follow the letter 'L:' Loss, Longing, Letting go, Love, Liberty, Life, and Leadership—or, Learning; or something like that. But what significance holds the letter 'L?' It's just a letter. Maybe I'll call them the **Little** *Things. But Life and Love and Loss and Liberty are not little things. No, not one of the latter could be thusly named! They're too important, too special, to be trivialized. Hmm, speaking of special, I wonder if Chachiano's is still having that special on stuffed shells. Yeah, but it's the meatballs that are the real Chachiano's treat. I'll tell you, those meatballs are sure—*

G.O.T.I.T™ *Brain Reader Deactivated*

That's it! Meatballs! That's the answer! That's what all of this has been about! Meatballs! Can't you see? It's so simple—how did I not think of it before just now?

Think about it: what is a meatball? Why, it's a balled concoction of meat, a handful of ground cow flesh, seasoned and rolled nicely into a delicious, cooked sphere, served alongside a meal that would otherwise, in and of itself, feel incomplete—which is basically any meal, in my book. Why confine yourself to only *spaghetti* and meatballs? Why not try *salmon* and meatballs, or *salad* and meatballs, or *peanut butter and jelly* and meatballs? See? They go with everything!

A meatball, like a collection of seven short stories, is packed with flavor, loaded with sustenance, and satisfying any time and every time, no matter what the occasion. A meatball, by its very spelling, is for **ME**, for **ALL,** and for everything in between—which, I suppose, in this case, if you were to juggle the remaining letters (A, T, and B), would be **BAT***s*? Or maybe it's everything from **A T**o **B**? Or those **AT B**, which could be a reference to a place called The B, I guess.

But, anyway, *meatballs*!

I'd mentioned them in the very beginning, having no idea just how significant they were to this overall compilation, or how prophetic my choice to use them in a light-hearted context would prove to have been.

Amazing.

Truly amazing.

And you know what else is amazing?

ANYONE WHO BOUGHT THAT!

Meatballs?

Are you *kidding*?

Did you really think I was going to end this book with the revelation that everything leading up to this point had been but single brushstrokes upon the canvas of a carefully crafted, metaphorical masterpiece, melding together into one giant ball of meat?

Perhaps it would have been fun (as I assume is the mindset of every contemporary conman—I'm sorry, I mean—"*crafts-man*" who sells blank, white canvases or strings tied from ceilings to art galleries, disguised as "art") to watch people debate how this concoction of literature really is like a meatball, how the spherical viand and it are alike in the most compelling of ways. Surely the authoritative position of author and the trusted seat of narrator could convince the masses that something profound has occurred, and thus leave them spellbound.

No.

There is no fun in deception, and I detest self-important expression, which gloats in its ambiguity, while hiding behind the guise of art and creativity to compensate for the curse of truly having nothing to say.

I have something to say, and so does the Author.

And so, let it be said.

What overall message does this collection hold? Very simply that you, dear reader, are here reading it; that you have chosen to invest your time and attention listening to the voice of another—his thoughts, his experiences, his ramblings. The point is not a message of surprise, like the revelation of a villain's identity, nor does it lie in a perspicacious statement, as would from the wise, old wizard be offered to the labored hero after a long journey. Instead, the real point, the true purpose of this book, lies in you.

We all have a story to tell, and you have sat here awhile and listened to ours, the Author's and mine; and possibly you have enjoyed our so-called "ramblings." What value our words have brought, how they have touched you, spoken to you, or even, should we be so blessed, inspired a change in your own narrative: this the point has ever been; and may the point ever be.

May you take from these tales—and from my own, waggish tongue—a blessing that will enrich the tale you, dear reader, have yet to tell. We pray that you will find peace in loss, fulfillment for your longing, strength to let go; that you will love unabashedly, without bounds; that you will protect and preserve liberty, learn from the past, and lead into the future; and that you will ever live for something greater than yourself.

But most of all, may you **NEVER** ramble.

Honestly, *The Ramblings of a Small-Town What's-His-Name* is just a title, one that had come to the Author whilst driving, long before penning a single word printed herein—long, even, before my employment. It was his hope that some day he could use the title for a collection such as this; but that word, *Ramblings*, though it worked so nicely as a title in a vacuum, he feared did not work with the content or message.

While you, dear reader, may feel differently, that what you have read is nothing more than a confused and inconsequential collection of babblings (thus, "ramblings" is right on the money), not one stroke of the pen printed herein was not deliberately made, nor was a single thought or idea idly crafted. Whether or not you agree with or appreciate those thoughts and ideas, whether or not anything you have read has touched or resonated with you: these will be up to you to determine. The Author and I have made our honest introductions—*give us your hands, if we be friends.*

It would be injudicious of me not to address this rambling business—and perhaps it's injudicious *not* to just amend the title. But, seeing as I am just the narrator, who cannot hope to sway the stubborn will of his employer, let me encourage you thusly:

Do not prattle or prate; rather, lift your voice with purpose and with passion. Forsake the unthinking, idle tongue, fit for the fools and the willingly enslaved, and lift a purposeful, pragmatic, and perfervid sound. And remember that we are not wise simply because we claim to be so, or because the world praises or reviles our words; and beware those who insist their own confused and rejected tongue is in fact the tongue of a wise man, unheard and misunderstood by the benighted of his time. The wise are quick to listen and slow to speak; they admit when they do not know; they accept when they are wrong, and thereafter seek the right; they are eager to study, to improve, to understand; they take the words and ideas of others as educational opportunities, as chances to examine a new ideology or view, and test an existing one by flame, or to simply better understand the mind of another.

You have attended to the Author's "ramblings," to mine; you have considered the thoughts and ideas of another with an open ear and an open mind. May the world ever be so gracious to you. We may not agree or enjoy what is from one another lifted, but may we never cease to lift our voices, share our stories, and offer our ideas to be challenged, as we—in the name of friendship, for the purpose of understanding, and in the pursuit of absolute truth (never our own brand)—challenge the thoughts and ideas of others.

And may you ever have a story to tell, dear reader.

May you tell it with passion and with purpose.

We'll be listening.

Farewell,

Your Faithful Narrator

THE END

Author Bio

C. K. Conners was born sometime, somewhere, and is still alive elsewhere. He is known by some as a hopeless romantic, a wearying wit, a formidably fluent fantasist, but most of all, *Who?*

When he's not writing about himself in the third person, this *what's-his-name* can be found flying in his private jet to exotic places, wine tasting with international business moguls, or philosophizing in robes and sandals on the steps of academia with fellow, curious-minded pupils—or, to put it more accurately, one can usually assume with confidence that on any given day Conners is locked in his room, wearing holey sweatpants and tattered moccasins, rocking a bedhead hairdo that would make Einstein jealous, sitting hunched over a blank piece of paper, and carving thereon the chicken scratch hieroglyphs he hopes to one day pass off as novels.

If he were, in any way, an interesting person, perhaps more than this could be relayed. But, alas, he is about as common as a scraped knee, and equally agreeable.

Route 27 Publishing

Founded in April 2018 by author C. K. Conners, Route 27 Publishing® and its children's books imprint Randy Boy Books® feature exclusively the literary madness produced by its founder, CEO, and bearer of basically every other company role. Though presently comparable in earnings to a not-for-profit organization, Route 27 Publishing® aims to one day grow large enough to employ full-time its founder, CEO, etcetera, etcetera, and bring into the public light all the tales he so desires to tell before his journey comes to an end.

An Imprint of Route 27 Publishing®

www.ingramcontent.com/pod-product-compliance
Lightning Source LLC
Chambersburg PA
CBHW032143170626
46808CB00006B/2348